Here are t...., ..g ... ., ...
a woman and a girl and sometimes a little bit of both. Andrea Rinard expertly plucks the key moments of her characters' lives and presents them to the reader like tiny, tough, perfect offerings. Life and death, carnations and ashes, love and loss, sirens and hamsters, it's all here. Rinard's prose is as sure-footed as it is wise, and this collection makes it clear that she's a writer to watch.

~AMY SHEARN, author of
Unseen City and other novels

In *Murmurations*, Andrea Rinard puts on full display the sheer range and craftsmanship of her writing. These are stories of and about girlhood and womanhood, the dangers and discoveries, the secrets and betrayals, and the things we trade for love. Within these works, Rinard is formally playful and inventive, as seen in "U-Pick" and "To-Do List," employing fragmented and breathless paragraph structures, while also employing mythical, magical, and speculative elements. There are lines and images here so sharp and rich and surprising they stopped me in my tracks: An old man who resembles "a melting candle where he leans against the wall." A woman who'd been taught "never to leave the house without lipstick or shame." The "language" of murmurating starlings. A strong collection of beautifully written, memorable stories, *Murmurations* is not to be missed.

~KATHY FISH, author of
Wild Life: Collected Works

Andrea Rinard's *Murmurations* fills the reader's mind with an aching silence often shattered by the slamming of lockers, the cracking of hearts, and the shouts of the too often ignored. In these stories. you find "the hard corners" of moments broken free from the monotony by fierce women characters who are brimming with life and vigor. Rinard commands our full attention, each story a perfect bauble of distilled life full of smells and truth, a sensory experience that soothes and challenges us from the first page. Rinard doesn't make it easy to look away from these characters with her clear and resonant prose. In *Murmurations*, she illuminates our secrets and feeds them back to us one sparkingly event after another. If you want to feel something, to see the world again in all of its glory and heartbreak, start reading this book!

~TOMMY DEAN, author of *Hollows*

MURMURATIONS

Andrea Rinard

Murmurations
Andrea Rinard

© 2023

All Rights Reserved.

FICTION
ISBN 978-1-958094-30-3

BOOK DESIGN • EK LARKEN
COVER DESIGN • MARGARET YAPP & ALANA SOLIN

EastOver Press encourages the use of our publications in educational settings.
For questions about educational discounts, contact us online:
www.EastOverPress.com or info@EastOverPress.com.

PUBLISHED IN THE UNITED STATES OF AMERICA BY

EASTOVER
— PRESS —

ROCHESTER, MASSACHUSETTS
www.EastOverPress.com

To all my students, past and present. Write on.

CONTENTS

LOVEBUGS

Maddi Mitchell has three lovebugs in her hair. One is poised on the edge of a golden curl cupping her left eyebrow. One is burrowed into the dark space behind her ear, its orange head peeking out like a signal fire. And one is perched on Maddi's part, and I imagine it grabbing two strands of hair like reins and riding her scalp all day.

I will gently pick them off, making sure not to crush them and smear death grease and release the smell like bell peppers and rotten potatoes. I will make a joke, so she won't be embarrassed even though Maddi never gets embarrassed about anything and even though lovebugs get everywhere so there's no reason to be embarrassed about having three of them in your hair anyway. Still, I heard her squealing yesterday in the courtyard before school when one flew too close, and she flailed away, the one and only time I ever saw her be anything but graceful and perfect. She will appreciate me for removing them. She will see me.

She will smile and say *thanks, girlfriend,* and we will walk together to fourth period. She will tell Brian Swilley to sit somewhere else and point to his vacated desk, and I will sit next to her. She will lean secrets on her elbow, twisted back in her seat to whisper to me when Mr. Carter isn't looking.

When the bell rings, we'll walk to the cafeteria. I'll sit next to her, and she'll admire my bento boxed lunch with the turkey roll-ups, sliced fruit, cheese cubes, and black olives all in their own little sections. I'll shrug and offer her a piece of pineapple. She'll ask if I understand what we're doing in geometry. I'll show her how to do the proof from today's lesson, and she'll say, *now I get it!*

I'll hang out at her house on the weekend, and her dad will have a nickname just for me, and her mom will have Múre Pepino LaCroix in the fridge because she'll know it's my favorite. Her little sister will ask me to help her with her homework, and her older brother will ignore me but secretly want to kiss me.

There will be pictures of us in the yearbook laughing together at the homecoming dance and at the spring service project. Everyone will know we're best friends, and they'll say, *MaddiandAnna* as if it's one word.

"What are you staring at, you freak?"

Maddi Mitchell is looking at me, her mouth twisted up and her eyes full of all the things I think about myself when I'm alone in my room, wishing I had somewhere else to be and someone to be with. I lift my hand slowly and move it toward her, all the things we'll do together held between the fingers that reach out to pluck the first lovebug from her hair so I can hold it out to her, an offering she will immediately understand.

"Don't touch me, loser."

Everything falls and shatters as the lovebug riding atop Maddi Mitchell's head tugs the reins and wheels her away, and I'm left with my empty hand still suspended in the air.

Sixth Period

We know where the hard corners are. We crouch together, our breaths slowing down while our hearts race, but we are quiet, quiet, quiet, quiet. If we are still and silent it'll be over soon, and we can get back to Hamlet's indecision and the Civil War and the laws of multiple proportions and *espero, esperas, esperamos.*

Jake is next to Moira. She smells like an apple made of jasmine, and he tries to scrunch himself in tight so his leg isn't pressed against hers because they don't know each other like that. Becca is staring at the poster on Mrs. West's wall that says, "Live as if you were to die tomorrow. Learn as if you were to live forever." She rolls Gandhi's words around in her mind like a marble until the words stop meaning anything at all. Paul wants to check his email because his SAT scores should be posted today, and he just needs fifty more points, but he knows better than to pull out his phone because that's not allowed. Anna forgot her lunch at home, and her stomach rumbles. Sergio looks at her and smiles. He will give her his leftover bag of pretzels as soon as the all-clear sounds.

Mrs. West watches the door, looking for the shadows to pass under it. The window facing the hallway has a laminated black paper cover that was distributed at the beginning of the school year along with the new and improved security plan. One per classroom. The directions for the black paper curtain are on page twelve, and "make sure every bit of the window is completely covered" is in bold.

Below that is a song to the tune of "Three Blind Mice," that's recommended for pre-K through 3rd grade. "Run, hide, fight. Run, hide, fight." Mrs. West thinks of her own children and wonders who they crouch with when they practice, when they rehearse what to do. Tears rise in her eyes, and she blinks hard. The doorknob rattles, and even though it's just the administrators checking the doors to make sure they're locked, making sure they can't see anyone through the windows, it scares her. She closes her eyes.

We crouch together, and it'll all be over soon. From when the alert is issued to the announcement that it's over, it may only be four minutes, but there are lifetimes in those seconds where we hide. We wait until we're told we can stand up and get back to normal. For now, though, we're in a hard corner, and no one can see us.

THE THIRD DATE

Beer splattered onto Gabby's lap where the cup landed, making a spot on her jeans that looked like nothing so much as a pants-peeing.

"Hey!" Josh jumped up, facing the beer-spiller who'd been jamming his knees into Gabby's back for the last inning. Now, she was wet and smelled like last call on their third date: burgers at Goody-Goody and a Rays game.

"You spilled beer on my girlfriend!"

All Gabby heard was "girlfriend." He was a nice guy, and she guessed she liked him, but how did meeting for coffee, going to a movie, and now a baseball game translate to a committed relationship?

"It's okay." She reached for his hand but missed as he raised it in the air and pointed a finger at the drunk man. "Just sit down."

Josh shouted at the drunk man while the drunk man's drunk wife tugged on his sleeve as he yelled back at Josh. "C'mon, Doug. Don't start this," the wife said.

Gabby'd swiped right and agreed to meet Josh because his picture was cute, and his profile made him out to be a good enough guy. Earlier tonight, however, she had brought up a political headline and realized that he didn't know the difference between the House and Senate. He ate hunched over with his elbows on the table, one arm curled as if protecting his fries. When she'd asked about his favorite book, he'd said, after a long hesitation, "I guess *How to Kill a Mockingbird.*"

He used too much product in his hair. It felt crunchy. She found that out at the end of date two when she'd experimentally tried to run her fingers through it while they kissed. And the kissing was not promising. His tongue was clumsy, and he'd held her waist like they were eighth graders at a dance.

As security raced up, Josh drew back his arm and released it like a piston into the drunk man's face. There was a meaty *thunk* then a silence until the drunk man launched forward. He and Josh flailed and fell on the two rows of people below.

One officer dug Josh out by the waistband and pinioned his arms behind him. Another heaved out the drunk man. Wrists were zip-tied, and they all marched down the stairs.

"Are you coming? Just follow me!" Josh called over his shoulder. He looked scared.

Gabby watched him disappear as the crowd applauded their exit.

Gabby looked back at the wife who seemed not really drunk after all. She looked directly into Gabby's eyes.

"I'm so sorry, honey."

"It's okay. Are you staying? Do you want to sit with me?" Gabby asked. The wife took the empty seat next to Gabby.

"Sorry about your boyfriend." The wife studied the scoreboard as the crowd started up a new chant.

"He's not my boyfriend," Gabby said, clapping her hands along with the crowd.

ELEVEN DAYS AFTER
THE HURRICANE

"You wanna watch out for them ants, babydoll."

The old man looks like a melting candle where he leans against the wall. It's a windless day with the air as thick as a hand across my mouth and nose, yet the geezer's having trouble lighting his cigarette. I decide to ignore him as I pick my way from the exit to the flooded Walmart parking lot, clutching my plastic bag that holds all I was able to grab inside the store: a two-liter of Diet Mountain Dew, five king-sized 3 Musketeers, and a bag of generic barbeque chips. They still don't have any bottled water or real food that doesn't need electricity to be edible. I should have been happy with what I got.

"You gon' be sorry, gal, you keep walkin' that way."

I stop and look at the brown water around my ankles and throw a confused glance over my shoulder before I think to stop myself. I don't want to get into a conversation or anything, but he catches my eyes and straightens up to stride over to my side. He's not actually a total wreck of a human but just a filthy, sweating man of anywhere between sixty and eighty with nowhere else to be.

"Look there." He points a calloused finger with grime caked beneath the nail. I follow the finger to a volleyball-sized hump on the surface of the water. I draw my left hand up to shade the sun. The hump is moving, pulsing.

"That there's an ant ball. Fire ants. You rub up 'gainst that, and you gon' be shakin' ants out your britches and wishin' you listened to me, gal."

I stare at the gathering that beats like the squeeze of an internal organ, the ants moving in all directions at once—up, around, and through their own mass. If I stepped in the middle of them, would they open a portal and usher me through? Or would I be covered by the ants and taken along with them, floating and throbbing in the oil-slick water?

I can feel the promise of hairy legs on my bare skin, moving under my t-shirt, across my stomach. All those bites at once would be like needles of fire, a baptism of pain that would deliver me from the hot, dark house with the line of black mildew on the walls, three feet from the warped floor where a quilt and three beach towels cover up the moist, stinking heap of everything that was ruined but can't yet be hauled away.

"Them ants," the old man's voice is close, "they's just lookin' for somethin', someone to grab ahold of."

The bottom of my bag breaks, and the soda, chips, and candy bars splash out, popping the spell like a bubble. I step back. *I know just how they feel,* I think, making a careful path away from the ants, leaving everything behind me in the fetid water.

BURNING

On the night before she started high school, Katelyn set the book on the grill. A scrape. A flash of orange. A whiff of sulfur. The corner caught, and the edges of the pages glowed. Aunt Ninny had given her the diary for her thirteenth birthday, saying with a wink, "A girl needs a place for her secrets."

She wrote in it, for the first few months, like it was a homework assignment, listing what she'd had for lunch, what the popular girls wore, what boys she liked, and how many times her dad didn't come home for dinner. The writing tapered off to once a week and then maybe once a month until May of eighth grade. She'd wanted to remember everything about those last three weeks before summer break, her script tightly packed into the spaces between blue lines, thick with details.

How the boy in the red baseball cap who sat in the back of the bus smiled at her. How his eyes started landing on her and sticking. How one day he didn't follow his friends to their seats. How he'd perched on the edge until she scooted over and made room for him. How he went three blocks out of his way to walk her home. How it started as kissing.

It ended with Dad coming home early, or maybe late, on a Wednesday afternoon and finding her on her knees with handfuls of the boy's jeans in each fist. Her mouth and eyes were salty as the boy ran out the back door, and Dad moved like his own shadow to the hallway, away from her. They never talked about it. Not like the boy who returned to the back seat of the bus and told the others things that made their lips twist, their eyes hooded and knowing. They watched her cheeks burn for those last days until summer.

The pages of the diary curled in on themselves and turned to a black square that shrank and flaked chunks of ash. Sparks flew, and she wondered if she'd set the trees on fire. For more than a moment, she wanted to burn everything to the ground, but she just scraped the last sheets of blackened paper until they disintegrated. Later, her father didn't tell her goodnight when she passed him on the stairs. She washed her hands. Scrubbed the soot that wouldn't come off. Avoided her own eyes in the mirror. The pages were gone, but she was still the girl who'd done those things because she'd wanted a boy to hold her hand.

MONSTER

I'm turning in front of my mirror like a jewelry box ballerina when I hear those blunt fingers of hers tap on the wood-that's-not-wood of my bedroom door. Mom knows better than to just walk in.

"Mandy? Everyone's waiting."

She would have liked to zip me up, to poke at my hair. I did let her drive me to the salon this afternoon and pay for it all. She sat in the waiting area, thumbing through old magazines, while the mirrors threw my reflection back and forth between them, an image of an image of a face. But there's nothing now for her to do. I'm ready.

I palm the little purse I had dyed with my shoes, red as blood, and open the door. Mom puts her hand to her throat like she's going to choke herself, but she's smiling. "You look so pretty."

I reward her with a kiss on her cheek, holding my breath so I don't get a noseful of her face cream which smells like wrinkles and the wrong kinds of flowers. She straightens the skinny strip of a strap that holds the top of my dress, so it lies flat at the tip of my collarbone, and I'm

Phoebe Cates coming out of the pool as I stride into the living room.

Four pairs of eyes meet me in the doorway. Dad's probably wishing there was less skin and more material. Tiffany's got to be second-guessing her pickle-green sequined dress with that asymmetrical long sleeve and the other shoulder bare. Chad's probably wishing she had a dress like mine and the body to go with it. Jeremy's hair is cut too short, too fresh, like a shaved dog, but his eyes move across every inch of my skin. An acceptable response.

I'm the last one to be picked up. Tiffany and I planned it that way because my backyard has a little white gazebo where we can take pictures. Tiffany was the one who'd brokered dates for us during Spanish III two days before Prom tickets went on sale. She passed notes to Chad who slipped them to Jeremy until Jeremy angled in his seat when Senora Gutierrez was writing vocabulary words on the board: *cautela, peligro, hambriento*. He glanced my way before shrugging and nodding at Tiffany.

Jeremy is adequate. He has a weird face, like someone took the chin, nose, eyes, mouth, and eyebrows from much more handsome faces and jigsawed the pieces together. A Frankenface. He has a red tie and cummerbund that aren't the right shade, but the corsage he's holding out is perfect. The rosebuds are a deep, rich, secret red with petals clutching their center as if they'll never open. When he slides it on my wrist, I see his blotchy-pink neck, and there is a shred of paper with a dot of blood under his jaw. A whisper of tenderness brushes against the inside of my chest. For tonight, totally adequate.

The dusk is mosquito-humid, and Tiffany and I tiptoe so our heels don't sink into the grass. Mom poses us on the steps, and Dad snaps photos one by one between the clicking countdown of him advancing the film. Jeremy and Chad on the top step, Tiffany and I right below. Then all of us in a sideways line, our chins tipped to the right. Then we stand inside the gazebo, leaning against the rail, the boys resting their sweating hands on our waists.

The line of Jeremy's body pressing against mine isn't new. The four of us already went skating two times and bowling once. Two other times it was just Jeremy and me in his dad's Chrysler LeBaron convertible on our way to a movie or dinner at Steak 'n Shake. I'd let my hair whip in my face so I could close my eyes and pretend I was flying. We kissed four times, his tongue so timid and testing I had to remind myself not to bite.

At the limousine, I get in first and push myself against the corner so Jeremy will see my chest pushed up and my legs framed by the slit of my dress. But he and Chad tumble in like puppies, and Jeremy drops into the seat without looking at me. He's too busy clicking the lights on and off above the windows, switching the radio station to KICK 98.5, and opening the mini fridge to peer inside.

"We should've brought something better to

drink," he says, pulling out a can of New Coke.

"I don't know why they had to change it," Tiffany says, getting one for herself and cracking it open.

"I wish we had rum." Chad gets one too, and the three of them start debating the merits of the new and old Cokes, their voices turning into strings that knot and snarl until I angle to the window. My silhouette is etched against the darkness, and I tip up my chin a little so I can see myself better from the sides of my eyes. The commercial on the radio ends, and Don Henley's singing about how all I want to do is dance. I close my eyes, and I'm alone in the limo, on my way to a party where a man with a smudge for a face will hold out his hand to help me rise from the car. Everyone's eyes will find me. Everyone will want me. Everyone will—

"Mandy, c'mon."

I'm alone, and the music is gone. It's Jeremy by the door, and we're here. I emerge like a dark dawn, and I'm every one of Molly Ringwald's happy endings. I'm Samantha blowing out her candles with nothing to wish for. I'm Andie in her pink dress, hearing Blane say, "I love you... always." Except my dress is red, but we're holding hands, and the regular people staying at the hotel are stuck in their roles as extras, watching as we step into the lobby.

The floor is a black and white tile that seems to sink in the middle like I'll drop into the floor and disappear if I walk over it. Like that perspective exercise we did last year in art class.

My stomach turns over, but I keep walking to the ballroom where music pulses and lights lick the edges of the doors. I clutch Jeremy's hand and keep my eyes up. An elderly couple passes us, and I straighten my spine and smile. They have to know their eyes are following something brighter than any other light. They're wilting flowers turning toward a sun they can't keep.

A sign welcomes us: *Welcome Roosevelt High Class of 1988 Prom!!!* Chad opens the door for Tiffany, but Jeremy drops my hand and follows them in without waiting for me. I follow, boring pits into the back of his skull until we line up for pictures in front of the balloon arch. We're AmandaJeremyTiffanyChad, baring our teeth for the photographer. There's another world somewhere where this moment is enough, but I don't live there. I imagine a string through my spine that comes out the top of my head. I pull that string and balance on my toes until I'm taller than Jeremy. He'll hate seeing those inches in the pictures, hate looking like a mortal next to a glowing goddess. He should have held the door for me.

Tiffany runs to the dance floor as "You Spin Me Round" starts banging. I whirl behind her, and we're holding hands, jumping to the beat. Jeremy will be watching, and I can feel his eyes moving across my skin as I twist, my arms above my head. When I start spinning with the chorus, though, he's laughing with Chad, and they're talking to another boy and that girl Becca from trigonometry class.

She has a perfectly smooth blonde bob that makes my own shellacked crown of curls feel like an ugly hat. Her dress is what Mom would call an LBD, a form-fitting black sheath that stops a couple of inches above her knees with a modest little slit to expose her tan thighs, muscled from cheerleading. The neckline is a promise rather than a demand, and I glance down at the shelf of my own cleavage, rising and falling as I pant. Becca's leaning into Jeremy, touching the spot below his elbow because he's already peeled off his tuxedo jacket and rolled up his sleeves. She's tiny. Like a doll I could snap the head off.

"What's wrong?" Tiffany screams by my ear, and I twirl to face her, my grin as convincing as always. I grab her hands in answer, and we're dancing again.

Three songs later, the beat fades into a slow dance, "Lady in Red." Chris de Burgh. I listened to it over and over the summer before junior year. It's the song in the background of the fantasy I crafted of double-dating with my best friend to Senior Prom. I'd be the lady in red, the one that made everyone hold their breath. I won't go to him. He'll know. But Jeremy is balancing a spoon on his nose, his head tipped back, his throat a long arc above his unbuttoned collar. Becca is laughing next to him, and my mouth fills with the hot thickness of my saliva.

I don't leave the square of swaying couples right away. Chad is heading toward us, coming to claim Tiffany. He shoves Jeremy on his way, but instead of following behind Chad, Jeremy bends to retrieve the spoon and rubs it on the untucked tail of his shirt before positioning it back on his nose while I wait. But he's not coming. I actually have to walk off the dance floor while my song is playing, and I bump into him, hard, as I stalk past him to the lobby.

The black and white floor calls me again to its center where it waits to swallow me. I keep my chin up and my eyes forward. A couple walks by. They look like my parents but not as tired. He's in khakis and a collared shirt, and she has on a pink skirt and a white top with ugly ruffles that flatten her chest. They're probably going to the restaurant on the other side of the lobby. He'll order a steak and baked potato, and she'll get chicken. They both wear wedding rings, but maybe they're married to other people, here for a secret weekend. Maybe she'll leave claw marks on his back. Maybe she'll draw blood.

The man's eyes meet mine, and he smiles. I arch my back slightly, just enough to lock him in. The woman's eyes travel over my dress, and she must be thinking of things she's dressed up for, or maybe she's wondering if she ever looked this good. But then we're staring in each other's eyes from across the room. She tightens her narrow nude lips and hurries her steps, pulling the man behind her. She stabs a glance at me, and her face says, *mine*. Maybe she's like me. Maybe she smelled me coming.

Two boys and a girl scurry from the elevator toward the doors to the pool. The boys are maybe eight and ten, wearing swim trunks and flip-flops, their smooth torsos and skinny arms bare. The girl is older, probably fourteen. Her hair is skinned back into a high pony, and she's got a towel wrapped around her waist, just under her bikini top. She's hunched like some kind of prey when a woman in an ugly polyester uniform steps in front of her.

"You need to be appropriately dressed when you walk through the lobby. Bathing suits are only for the pool area and beach."

The girl nods to the floor and herds the boys back to the elevator. They disappear. If I watch for her, I might see her return in a few minutes with shorts and a t-shirt over her bathing suit. The boys, I know, would still be half-naked. No one will say anything about them.

My lips curl. She'll learn.

There's no one else to look at, so I stare directly at the squares on the floor until they start moving. I let my brain follow the pattern until my eyes unfocus, and I'm somewhere else. Time slides through me until a man's voice pulls me back. "Are you okay?"

My eyes adjust on the face in front of me, a face above a uniform. It's nice. The face, not the ugly uniform that looks like it itches. Nothing but normal. "The floor."

"Come sit down."

My heart beats through the sludge of the disorientation.

"You maybe having too much fun? Are you going to be sick?"

If I tell him what I do for fun, will he run

screaming, or will he sit next to me, lean closer, let me sniff the skin behind his ear?

"I can get you some water."

I shake my head and sit up straighter. I've never needed to be the damsel in distress. "I'm fine. That floor just made me a little dizzy."

"It's no problem. I'll be right back."

When he returns, I could ask him to walk outside with me. *I can use some fresh air.* He'd believe me. They always do. I could pretend to stumble and slither my hand around his elbow. He'd let my fingers stay tucked there, and we'd stand in a shadow with the voices of kids whose parents let them stay in the pool after dark behind us. *Marco! Polo!* He'd put his hand over mine, holding us together, and I'd be Claire pressing her diamond into Bender's palm. And then... and then...

But when he comes back with a glass of water, he passes through a blade of light, and I see where the skin will sag on his neck. The creases of time, not laughter, that will carve themselves around his eyes. The mediocrity. He's no Judd Nelson. He's not even a Jeremy.

I take a couple of polite sips and pass the glass back, careful not to let our fingers touch. "Thanks. I'm really fine." He's gone from my mind like an insect passing a tiger.

"What's going on?" Jeremy appears by my side. Tiffany probably told him to go after me, but it's too late.

"Let's walk on the beach."

"I don't know. My mom said not to. This tux

is rented." He clasps his hands, and the rasp of palm on palm is a locust rubbing its legs in a language I don't know. I speak a different tongue, one I know he'll recognize.

"I just wanted to be alone with you," I murmur into his ear, pushing my breasts against his upper arm. I take the soft lobe between my teeth and press. Just a little.

We leave our shoes in the sand by the boardwalk. Jeremy tucks his socks inside his, and I'm almost charmed. But the horizon swallowed the sun a while ago, and the sky is a thick black blanket drawn over us as we walk to the wet sand. There's no one else here as I lead him to the old pier that shadows from the water like a dark skeleton. It must have been damaged in a storm because it hunches up with no access point, a beheaded beast sinking with time. Still, there are places beneath it where a couple can lean against the splintery wood and make secrets.

I'm Baby, waiting for Johnny to lift me in the air so I can slide down his body. I'm Lana, telling Joel to take me on a real train. But Jeremy presses a soft kiss on the corner of my mouth. His hands rest on my waist like he's holding an egg with no impulse to apply the right pressure just to feel it crack open. I pull back slightly to study his eyes, brown as bread, as puppy fur, as an unlucky penny. A pimple bulges whitely in the crease of his nose.

There's a possibility he could change the course. He just needs to say something. He could tell me how much he wants me. How hot

I am. How he never wants this night to end. He turns and looks behind me, to the water.

"I wonder if we'll see any dolphins jumping."

And I can't stop myself.

~

The bottom of my Prom dress is wet and caked with sand. I loved this dress, but now, all I want to do is strip to the strapless bra and red satin underwear I'll never wear again. I want to heave the dress like the peel of a rotten banana into the salty blackness mouthing my toes. I shouldn't have done it. Not tonight. Not yet. But what else could I do? I should run as far as I can, making the sand squeak under my feet as my legs piston faster and faster. There's no one as far as I can see, though, so staying another minute is okay. But I have to be careful. Instead of sinking to my knees and howling, I settle for pulling the pins out of my hair.

Hairspray makes it hard to drag my fingers across my aching scalp, but I rip through the stiff curls, untangling the sprig of baby's breath the lady at the salon said was elegant. I hold it to my nose, but it smells like nothing. It lands where the pins fell.

I squint at the water, imagining I can see him, rising and falling with the tide at the end of the pier's shadow, just a place where the water is a little too dark. But there's nothing to see. It's done. I need to get back to the dance.

The music from the ballroom reaches me

across the expanse of beach like I'm holding a tin can on a string with the other end propped next to a radio. "Mony Mony." Billy Idol. Released 1981. Originally recorded by Tommy James and the Shondells in 1968. The beat stabs, and my jaw unclenches into an almost-smile as I stare at the hotel.

It has two wings on either side of the pool we passed. It looks like the building has a glowing eye on each side. *Monocular*. That's what Ms. Bishop called it in sophomore biology when a creature's eyes face out to the sides instead of forward. "Prey animals need monocular vision so they can watch for threats coming at them, but they can't see predators that approach head-on." Deer, lizards, rabbits... they're all food for bigger animals. Birds too, except owls. I saw an owl snatch up a rabbit once in a park right at sunset. It dropped like lightning and was gone before my heart knew to beat faster. The light from the dropping sun leaked orange through the branches of the trees where the owl took its meal.

But I can't let my thoughts fly me away. I need to go back inside, but I can't look like a girl who had bad things happen to her or did them herself. My hair's not wet, but it's a mess. I should have just tolerated the ache of the up-do. I shuffle my feet to find the bobby pins and only come up with four. I scrape back a few strands and secure them, hoping it looks like I've just been dancing so hard, having so much fun, that the structure it took an hour to erect couldn't hold.

My shoes are two embers burning in the sand, waiting for me. I hook my fingertips to carry the shoes and leave Jeremy's behind, faithful and solid with the socks still rolled inside. No one looks at me as I move through the lobby, the checkerboard pattern on the floor dizzying me even more until I get to the throbbing lights and a pulse of music that vibrates in my blood. I slip my shoes back on, and the grit of sand chafes into a sting that feels just right.

Tiffany bobs up next to me from the sea of bodies and screams, "Come dance!" She doesn't notice or at least doesn't ask where Jeremy is, and he shrinks down to fit inside the box in my mind where I keep things that used to be important. My whole body unhinges itself, and sweat slicks my back. Some of the boys are screaming along with the chorus, "Get laid, get fucked." I widen my legs to give the skin between my thighs a slippery gasp and then I'm dancing. The long muscles between hip and knee burn deliciously as I twist and spin. So beautiful.

If Mom and Dad could see me, they'd put their hands over the mouths of doubt that have been whispering to them for a startlingly long time. They'd forget that my eyes are blank flags, meeting theirs with no fidelity to the nationality of their love. They'll put a picture from tonight on the refrigerator of me and Tiffany and Chad and Jeremy. Our bland happiness could have soothed some of the itch under their parental skin if not for Jeremy. Still, they'll leave the picture up to prove to themselves there's no reason not to.

They'll never say out loud or even in the private places inside themselves how relieved they are I got accepted to a college too far to visit regularly. Their empty nest will feel so comfortable around them, and they will love me more honestly from a distance. Phone calls will ebb as quietly and steadily as stagnant water down a stainless-steel drain until they almost forget they have a daughter. Neighbors will ask for a while to be polite, and Mom will crease her forehead before my place in her life creeps forward. "Oh, Mandy's fine! Thanks for asking!"

I know all these things. I've always known.

Billy Idol's voice melds into Phil Collins and a girl that's been on his mind.

January 1985. I rewound the mixtape over and over, dancing to it in my room until the words were just noises that moved my body. Like now.

The beat is less vicious than "Mony, Mony," and everyone rocks from foot to foot in a steadier sea. Tiffany swings her arms and hips, but she's trying too hard. Her face is pinched in a concentration that lets me know she's posing, not dancing. A white-hot arc of hate flashes though me. I can feel my fingers locking into handfuls of her hair, yanking it out of her scalp, and watching the blood run down her face like melting crayons.

But Chad appears and yells something in her ear. I move my eyes to his lips to catch one word. *Jeremy*. Tiffany shrugs, grabs my elbow, and steers us to the exit, back into the lobby and the floor that calls to me, a siren song of black and white. I could drop to my hands and knees to crawl, my shoulder steadied against the wall, but that wouldn't be right. I look straight ahead and keep the pattern below the frame of my sight.

"Do you know where Jeremy is?" Chad is still yelling. I picture a train, barreling toward us, its horn blasting, but Tiffany clutches my elbow.

"Mandy, where'd he go?"

We could go out to the beach, sit with our dresses hiked over our knees, squeezing sand between our fingers, look for the place in the dark where Jeremy used to be. I'd want to tell her straight like rain, but there are no words. I'd end up asking questions. Does it make you tired to wear that face? What do you love? Who the fuck are you?

"We walked for a little bit, but I wanted to come back. I guess he kept walking." Simple stories are always best. I pull the blankness of my face around me, and Tiffany and Chad keep talking. I let myself float away from their voices, back to the water. It would be warm like amniotic fluid. Or blood. Is he scuttling across the bottom? Or is he moving in some kind of jellyfish ballet, the currents taking him to a secret place? "So beautiful," I whisper softly, but saying it out loud snaps me back. I have to pay attention.

Tiffany and Chad are still talking. Important

business. A conference. "Should we go look for him?"

"What did you do? Maybe he's pissed off." Chad's eyes try to pin me in place, but he has nothing sharp enough for that sort of thing.

"He'll come back sooner or later," Tiffany says, choosing her allegiance. There's no memory of anger in my body as I link my arm in hers, pressing my skin against her loyalty, marking her with my scent.

Mr. Pennock's words from AP Lit bounce like a rubber ball in my mind. "Dramatic irony is when the audience knows something the character doesn't, creating tension, suspense, or even a sense of the ridiculous." I turn my laugh into a cough. It's going to be a long night.

What's coming next runs in a reel, my own personal cinema. In the opening scene, the lights will come up, and Jeremy will still, of course, be gone. Chad, or maybe Tiffany, will go to one of the adults, one of the People in Charge. There'll be a search, but they'll never find him. I'm good at that. Someone will ask me for Jeremy's phone number. Everyone will assume I'm too upset to remember what I never bothered to memorize, but Chad will recite it as Tiffany rubs a circle on my back. The police will come. Everyone will ask me *but what happened?* with their arms crossed, their hands clasped, their heads tilted.

Jeremy's parents will run in. They'll stay long enough to get what crumbs of information the police have to offer before going out to the beach. Jeremy's name will streak across the sand as his mother calls to the north and his father to the south. They'll know he's out there. They're positive they'll find him, lead him back. They'll take him home and put him to bed like a toddler. They're sure of that. But long after I'm gone, they'll still be looking. They'll always be searching for him.

I'll have to call Mom and Dad because the limo driver will have left. They'll rush into the office where Tiffany, Chad, and I will be sitting. They'll ask me the same questions, sure I saved some tidbit, some morsel of information just for them. Tiffany and Chad's parents will come, and the questions will bounce against a wall and head back toward me. We'll finally leave with the pale threat that *someone will be in touch*. Mom and Dad will keep asking me things, their questions looping around and doubling back before crashing into my answers. *I don't know. I don't know. I don't know.*

They will watch me walk to my room, listening for the soft click of the door between us. I'll think about Jeremy the next time I do it, knowing I'm getting better and better. This time will just be a Bad Thing that happened at Prom. It will be something everyone will whisper about at graduation when they pass the empty seat the principal will keep for Jeremy at the ceremony. Then everyone will let him drift away. *What was that guy's name? The one that just disappeared?*

Days will go by. Then weeks. Months. Mom and Dad will never say out loud the things they're thinking, the thoughts that burrow like larvae.

They'll never believe what I already know, what I've always, always known.

Bouquets

The man in the parking lot handed her a pink carnation. Sara accepted what the stranger offered as unconsciously as taking a spoon to put away when she used to help Mother do the dishes. The man smiled and kept going across the asphalt that shimmered in the late afternoon heat.

Sara clutched the long green stem. What was she supposed to do with it? She had been similarly bemused when Will Engleman brought a trembling fistful of multicolored carnations when he picked her up for their first, and next to last, date while she was home from college the summer before her sophomore year. Mother had shooed her into the kitchen to get a vase— not the good crystal one—following her behind the closed door to remark that carnations were cheap trash flowers.

Three weeks ago, Sara had wrapped up that good vase, heavy as an anchor, in newspaper and put it in the box marked for Goodwill along with the rest of Mother's things. She didn't need another empty thing in her empty house.

A little lightheaded from the heat, Sara leaned her hip against the sensible Toyota John had picked out for her. He'd said she could drive it forever as long as she remembered to change the oil. John was always right; she no longer had the husband, but the car still ran great.

John never brought flowers home to her, had never sent them to her office as a surprise. Mother said more than once, "They just die," meaning, Sara guessed, flowers were a waste of money. But that would make everything a waste.

But Mother had too much of an interest in flowers when Sara and John planned their wedding. Sara wanted the peonies, drooping under the weight of their own beauty. Clusters of hydrangeas that looked like mobs of butterflies. Carnations as pale pink as a single layer of a ballerina's tutu.

Mother insisted on the stern, wax-white calla lilies and roses so red they looked more like the idea of a rose than a rose. Sara walked down the aisle next to her silent father, holding the bouquet her mother had proclaimed "so elegant" but reminded Sara of a circus tent. She'd held it steady under her chin, wishing, not for the first or last time, she could have something that was hers alone, longing for the smell of carnations.

In the parking lot, Sara held the flower as she imagined one would a dirty diaper. She marched toward the garbage can by the entrance to Publix with the idea of hurling the flower into the trash with a satisfying downward motion of her arm, like a gesture that would accompany the refutation of an undeniably false statement.

She paused with the carnation shoulder-high and looked at the electric doors as they opened for another customer, swooshed closed, and then opened again. Sara touched the fleshy ruffles of the carnation to her nose, breathing deeply. It smelled like everything that could be just for her.

ENTROPY

I need to make myself smaller. I need to not take up so much space. I suck the oxygen out of the house, this family. I'm busy shrinking myself when she comes into the only room in the house with empty hinges.

Mom has those eyes, and I know she's about to say again *(and again, and again)* "Did you take your meds?"

Yes. It's always *yes.* I swallow the pills every morning, round like a buoy. I do what I'm supposed to do even though nothing keeps me afloat.

Those eyes walk away, but they've rent my skin, and I seep, the blood rising. I try to unfurl my wings to fly away because the window still works, but my wings arc sticky, and I can't rise. A single feather falls. More will follow unless I'm very still, so I fold in on myself and try not to look up.

~

I need to make myself smaller. I need to not take up so much space. There's not enough space, enough air for me in this house, in this family. Mom walks though the doorway to the open portal to where I live, the only room without a door.

Her eyes swallow me, and she digests me in a glance; I'm getting better at being small.

"Did you take your meds?"

I nod because I need to take away the sadness, a darkness over the hope and the love. If I'm smaller, I won't cast a shadow.

Besides, it's always *yes*. I swallow the pills every morning, but I'm still the heaviest thing in the house, in the world. I will sink us all. Mom's eyes say she knows, but she will always hold out her hand and let me drown her.

Mom's eyes walk away, and I look at my window. I will be able to fly away, far, far, far, and Mom's eyes won't see me. I imagine I have wings, but I'm not a bird. I'm an anchor. My only view is the bottom, and I will sink down, down, down.

~

I need to make myself smaller. I need to not take up so much space. I am a vacuum taking every breath meant for others. Mom pauses where my door used to be.

They all stop when they pass, but Mom is the one whose eyes hurt. She asks me in the only language we now speak, "Did you take your meds?"

Yes. It's always *yes.* The pills are round like a seashell, but I can't hear my own voice no matter what I press my ear to.

Mom walks away, and I'm tired. So, so tired.

I think of sun. The beach. A single gull circling the sky. I want to find that child who collected shells, holding them out to her mother who put them in a bucket like treasure. It's too far away to see clearly, but I keep looking out the window.

THE HANDS REMEMBER

Isit on the bench outside Publix. Seconds ago, a little boy ran by me in light-up sneakers when I was almost, almost, almost to the door, and suddenly I could hear Caleb's feet, encased like two meat loaves in the shoes I got him before he started K-3, drumming against the cart. He was so careful not to kick me after that one time— *Don't hurt Mommy!*

I'd had to let go of the cart and sit down because everything was narrowing down to a tunnel with Caleb at the other end. I tried to count my breaths, and I told Tom to *just go, just go,* and he didn't ask what the trigger was. He just went through the sliding doors into the grocery store.

I hold the memory the way Caleb's chubby fingers would grip the handle of the cart, my fingers closed around themselves like a puzzle. Caleb used to crack himself up, asking for silly things for dinner. *I want toilet paper to eat! I'll eat it all!* And he'd cackle and I'd laugh and we'd putter around the store, doing the things that only the two of us in the whole world do, but now I'm doing the breathing stuff Dr. B suggested.

In. Out. In. Out. Feel your lungs expand. I can't

go in the store. *Can't. Can't. Can't.* Tom says *won't,* but it's not that. It's just a word, but it's a word he's pushing around with the cart right now, filling it with meals he'll prepare, and I won't eat, and I can feel his rage from where I'm sitting. I have no room for anger, though. The despair is too big and too heavy. There's no space for anything else.

It's been three months, he'd said.

Fifteen weeks and two days, I'd said.

His jaw did that thing that was new, like so many other things that were new since Caleb left. *Died,* Dr. B's voice shoves me, but I whisper *left.* I don't like the vocabulary I'm asked to use—words like *mindfulness, ruminative coping, adaptive grieving,* and *bereavement pathways*—so I don't. So stubborn. That's new too.

Something nudges my ankle, and I look down. There's a collarless little dog sitting at my feet, some kind of terrier mix. It looks like Toto but brown and not quite like Toto after all. It's looking up at me, and I recognize him immediately. If I hadn't been looking, I wouldn't have seen him. *Caleb,* I whisper, and the little dog wags his tail and lets me stretch my hands around his warm belly. I lift him to my lap where he perches like a toddler.

There's a fat tick under his left eye like a gray teardrop, and I pinch it off. All that stuff about matches and tweezers is unnecessary. You just have to know what to do, and my hands remember. Like holding a newborn with its head like a giant flower on a narrow stem or rubbing a nightmare-sweaty back exactly right or cutting a sandwich into two perfect, crustless triangles. It's been fifteen weeks and two days since they've had work to do, but my hands remember. As the dog and I gaze into each other's eyes, I know he remembers too. *Caleb*.

Tom doesn't know how to say no to me anymore, so the three of us go home together. Tom calls it a mutt, but Dr. B calls it an *affirmation of life*, so I win. She suggests so, so, so gently to find *a different name, a name that will represent this new chapter in your story*, but it's Caleb, and I don't even care how Tom winces every time I call the dog to me. I don't care how the house echoes with his anger. *It's just a dog!* But I know what's real.

He makes me choose after twenty-seven weeks and four days, and it's not a choice. I don't even need Dr. B anymore. Caleb and I sit on the couch together while Tom packs a bag. *I'll be at my parents' until I find my own place. I'll get the rest of my stuff after I figure out what I'm doing.*

I feel bad for him, but I already know what I'm doing. I gather Caleb in my arms, and he doesn't even wiggle much as I hold him tight against my breasts and rock back and forth, enjoying the silence with my little boy.

U-Pick

"You checked yourself out against medical advice?"

"I'm not drinking, Lex. I just passed out because it was hot."

"You shouldn't be out walking, Dad."

"Well, you didn't get my cigarettes!"

"Instacart won't deliver tobacco. I told you that."

"Mom! A bee!"

"It's just a fly, Chloe."

"I'll walk back to the hotel. It's only a couple of miles."

"Dad, call a cab. I'll give you a credit card number to use."

"Who are you talking to, Alexandra? Get the stroller out of the sun. Sam's feet are red."

"Is that your mother?"

"Is that your father? Is he drunk again? Just hang up."

"Why is she there? What are you doing?"

"We're picking blueberries with the kids."

"We used to do that—remember? You'd eat more than you'd put in your bucket."

"Just hang up!"

"Mommy! It really is a bee!"

"Mom, help Chloe. Dad, I'll send an Uber. Text me the hospital's address."

"I don't know the address."

"Ask someone! Dad?"

"Don't yell, Lex! I'm trying to find someone!"

"Just hang up. In Al-Anon, we—"

"3214 West Morgan Street."

"I need you to text it to me."

"My readers broke when I fell. It's easy—thirty-two like how old you are and fourteen for what comes after thirteen."

"I'm thirty-four, and you need to text it to me."

"Just hang up, Alexandra."

"I can't see to text! You can remember. 3214 West Morgan Street. You used to have a friend named Morgan, right?"

"I'm ordering the Uber, Dad. What's the hotel address?"

"It's the Best Western near the interstate."

"Ok, I guess I need to Google that."

"Moooooom! I got stung!"

"Mom, please help Chloe!"

"He's a grown man. You're enabling him. And Sammy's feet are definitely sunburned."

"Did Chloe get stung by something? Get a cigarette and make a spit-poultice with tobacco. Make sure you get the stinger out."

"I found the hotel address, Dad. Go to the main entrance and wait for the Uber. It's a guy named Sayid in a silver minivan."

"Where's the main entrance?"

"I have no idea! The driver's almost there."

"Do you think the guy will mind stopping by the Circle K so I can get my cigarettes?"

"Dad, I need to go. I've got another call. Call me when you're in the car so I know you're on your way."

"Mooooooom! It hurts!"

"I thought you said it was a minivan?"

"Just go to the main entrance, Dad. I've got another call. Hello?"

"Hello, yes, this is Sayid? The Uber driver? I'm at the address, but I don't see anyone.

"It's a hospital, right?"

"No, ma'am. The hospital is down the road."

"He must've got the address wrong. Can you go to the hospital? The main entrance?"

"If there's no one waiting, I'll have to cancel the ride."

"He'll be there. Thank you so much!"

I palmed my phone and pushed the stroller to where Chloe was holding her arm out like it was a bomb. An angry welt rose from the crease of her elbow.

"Mom, take Sam over to that bench in the shade."

"Is your dad okay? Why does he need a ride? Should I call him?"

"Mommy! It really stings."

I scooped Chloe up and buried my face in her damp neck, breathing in the smell of sweat, sun, and the clamminess of sunscreen. I carried her to the trough where the sign said, "Wash ur Hands!"

"I'm just going to check to see if the stinger is gone, Chloe. Hold real still."

My finger passed smoothly over the bump, and I held her arm under the water while she relaxed in my arms.

The phone vibrated in my pocket.

"Daddy?"

"Okay, honey, I'm with Sayid, and he's going to take me to get my smokes on the way. Thanks for saving me, baby. You kiss those kids for me!"

"Call me later, Dad."

Inside the little pole barn, it was breezy and cool. There were buckets of sweet corn, four for a dollar, and shelves of honey. The lady who'd handed us our buckets when we'd arrived tutted when she saw Chloe. Her pink apron had SUSAN embroidered on it in green thread.

"Did something get you, precious?"

"A bee."

"Hold still right there."

She got a bottle of honey from a shelf.

"Give me your finger, princess."

"It stung me on my arm."

"I know, pumpkin, but I'm going to put some honey on your finger, and then you put that finger in your mouth. There! Now, I'll put a gooey bit where that bee kissed you. Your sweet mama can put baking soda on it at home."

"Thank you. It's been a wild morning."

"Wild is what we mamas do best, right? You just go sit on my swing over there and let your little girl settle. Then you find your own peace."

When I scooted back on the wooden slats of

the swing, it eased back and forth like a sleepy cradle. Mom was giving Sam sips from a juice box, and Chloe was a melting weight against me. The boughs of the oak tree swayed, and the leaves shimmered where the sun touched them.

The heaviness of the morning rose behind my closed eyes and dissolved like sugar on my tongue. A wind chime dinged faintly, and Susan told someone how to make vegan blueberry cobbler.

I could stop answering Dad's calls, but he'd lifted me on his shoulders and walked down the rows, holding a palmful of blueberries for me to take one by one. I could be annoyed by her, but Mom used to make homemade whipped cream and hand me the beaters to lick. We'd spooned them into our mouths, those little blue worlds, topped with cream and tasting of summer.

My phone was silent, and I didn't have to do anything in that moment other than sit there with my daughter falling asleep in my lap, thinking of all the things there were to love.

MURMURATIONS

Mom's ashes are in the urn on the table, and I struggle to smile at people who hold pieces of her. I am greedy for every fragment, but hugs are extortion. We say we are putting her in the ground in a "private ceremony," but my dad keeps her next to the winter coats in the upstairs closet. He thinks there will be a right time.

~

Starlings cover the clouds. There is a language in the movement. It's called a murmuration, a colleague says as she passes, and it's the most perfect word for the wave that rises and dips and rises again. I find my hollow body swaying slightly as if holding a sleeping child in a moon-lit room, and I remember the songs my mother sang to me. Like a sheet lifted above a bed, the birds move across the sky.

~

The fat flakes covering the tarmac are fascinating to our Floridian eyes until we realize the guttur-al voice over the intercom announces all flights are postponed. We will miss our connection to

Moscow. My jaw is already sore, but I squeeze the panic into a wad behind my molars. My baby girl is waiting. In her picture, she has hair like down that will be so soft between my fingers. I wonder if my mother will see us. I rock uselessly back and forth. I wonder if my baby will smile when I gather her up. We've been waiting too long to meet her, to fill the space that's just for her. It's time to take her home.

~

A friend of a friend asks if I know anything about her real mother. My hands itch, fingers curl into talons that will rip her useless eyes out because she can't see. *Rise above it,* my mom whispers. *I am her real mother.* My daughter flies across the yard with her shoelaces untied and a necklace of dirt. Her beauty chokes me with its perfection.

~

Large, angry things stalk the house, and furious silhouettes with hooked beaks fly overhead. I move softly through the chronic outrage and try not to ruffle my daughter's feathers. Mom murmurs to me in the quiet of the sleeping house that it'll pass, that she survived my teenage years, that I'll be okay too. There's nowhere for a mother to hide anyway. I will ride the currents, waiting until my girl gives me a place to perch.

~

She's drinking her coffee over the sink with a cocked hip, her eyes raised to the almost-morning on the other side of the glass that reflects her darkly. She throws a half-smile to me over her shoulder, and I want to trace the shadowy crescents of delicate skin under the blueness that's nothing like my brown. She was up too late studying calculus. She rinses out her mug, and we're face-to-face, and I see her. We're both on firm footing, and all the questions burn away. Her smile is every answer. She will soar past the sun on wings I helped build.

To-Do List

Morning

Walk past his bedroom door and resist that tentative tap-tap-tap he hates and knows is just a prelude to you entering even if he doesn't say to come in. He'll be hunched in his bed. There will be a gathering of trash—empty chip bags, half-sipped bottles of water, and wads of tissue—on his nightstand. The sour stench of piled dirty clothes, unwashed skin, and unrealized potential will be almost more than your mother-heart can stand. The stuffed bear on the bed, the one he's held for nineteen years to help him fall asleep, will break you in pieces if you let it. Assure yourself that he'll get up and take a shower as soon as you leave for work.

Day

Don't text him that part-time job opening you Googled last night when you couldn't sleep. Don't call and ask if he submitted his paper online for freshman English, the one you "helped" him write. Don't remind him he can't retake the class if he fails again. Don't wonder if he's awake. If he's up. If he's showered. If he's eaten. Get through your day.

Evening

Walk past his bedroom door when you get home from work. You know he's in there. There's no need to ask in that faux-hopeful voice what he's accomplished today. You could go in and speak to him gently. You could put your hand on his shoulder, but your hand will offend the bird-like bones. It's the same hand that held his pudgy one when you crossed streets together, and your words are just words, and nothing is the same and everything is the same. He will murmur sleepily that he's just so tired and he's not hungry and he loves you and he'll try harder. You will have to force yourself not to slip under the covers to spoon against the man-child body that once curled like a shrimp below your breasts.

Night

Try again to convince yourself there's nothing you can do. That you're doing everything you can. Tomorrow will be better. You'll see your son again soon, the one you know is in there, buried beneath a weight you can't see, can't understand, can't lift. Don't tiptoe across the hall to stare again at the closed door. Stop crying.

MAGGIE

"Dolphins are carnivores." Maggie pushes her glasses up her slick nose and waits for the two other children building a sandcastle to look at her. They don't, but Maggie continues anyway. We've been at the beach on vacation for three days, and the little architects have already learned to ignore Maggie with exquisite brutality. "A full-grown dolphin can eat about thirty-three pounds of fish per day."

"Maggie, come let me put more sunscreen on you."

"I used the SPF 50 just..." she checks her watch, "Forty-seven minutes ago. I don't need to reapply for another forty-three minutes, Mom."

"Dolphins are very playful and highly intelligent." Maggie squats down by the sandcastle, and I see the boy whose name I've heard called across the sand, Stetson, cut his eyes at his sister whose name is either Cassie or Cassidy. They both look around Maggie's age, so they should all be playing together in the way temporary friendships are formed at the beach when the parents are watching from behind a book or phone. "Dolphins are very social, living in groups that hunt and even play together. Large pods of dolphins can have 1,000 members or more."

"Maggie, let's hunt for seashells." I try again, but she's picked up a handful of sand and is pressing it between her hands.

"Dolphins have acute eyesight and hearing."

"Maggie, it's almost time for lunch."

"Their sense of touch is also excellent."

"C'mon, Stetson. Let's go for a swim." They know Maggie will not follow them into the water, and they will stay there until we go back upstairs or until their fingers and toes wrinkle and their shoulders burn.

Maggie presses a handful of sand into the side of the castle and smooths the edges so no seams show. She stands and walks in circles, her head cocked to one side like a crow, until she finds a perfect cat's paw shell to place on the top of the castle before she returns to my side.

"Dolphins have few natural predators," she says, looking at Stetson and Cassie/Cassidy as they toss a ball back and forth in the water. "Their only enemies are humans."

Delayed Combustion

Mammaw burned up on Thanksgiving when I was thirteen. She was sipping an inch of bourbon, staring daggers at her "useless" daughters-in-law when she leaned over and said, "Chiclet, go over by your grandfather."

I'd smelled that whiff of blown-out match that came off Mammaw before, thick and heavy when she was angry, so I crossed the room immediately and perched behind Grampy's chair. Mom and Aunt Corkie kept talking about Jackie Kennedy. Aunt Corkie was wearing a pillbox hat, and Mom was dying to have one too even though Daddy voted for Nixon. He said Mom looked ridiculous, trying to curl her hair and wear gloves like the Papist first lady. The lot of them had been bickering all day. Mostly about the election, but the turkey was too dry, the Packers were beating the Lions, and the cranberry casserole wasn't right.

"You have the lava blood too, Chiclet." Mammaw had murmured her secret, and mine, in my ear one summer day between second and third grade as I got to my feet. My cousin Dip had pushed me down and walked over me, a giant striding past a cockroach. He was thirteen that summer, and I was only eight, a child-sized lifetime before Mammaw finally let it rip. I'd felt the sludgy fire moving through my veins as I watched Dip run off with the other cousins, never even looking back to see if I was okay.

"It'll eat you up, baby girl," she'd said, picking pine needles out of my hair. She'd taught me how to take deep breaths. How to count to ten, fifteen, twenty, five hundred. How to imagine a knob I could twist to turn the heat down, like a thermostat. How to feel the heat without letting it burn.

But she also whispered how one day, "a long time from now," I might want to, need to, fan the embers. I could blow on my anger until it raged. I could loosen my grip. "It won't hurt," she promised. "I know it won't hurt. Not more than a second anyway. It'll be like picking a scab, what you've been wanting to do for so long the pain'll feel good."

I wondered what could be so bad that could ever make me want the burning. I never got to ask Mammaw because she was glaring at Mom and Aunt Corkie, and then she looked right at me before closing her eyes. The air left the room so fast that no one else noticed, and then she was slumped to the side, with a wisp of smoke curling out of her ears.

I moved back to her side to touch her arm, to feel the heat. "Mother?" My dad knew something was wrong, but the knowledge hadn't risen to the surface of his brain yet.

"Charlotte, get back!" Dad waved his arms like flags, moving me aside as everyone else gathered around what used to be Mammaw. All the women cried out and fluttered into useless moths while Grampy gaped like a goldfish. I went and sat on the front steps, out of the way.

I was the only one who knew what she was capable of. I was the only one who knew she was a dragon whose fire stayed on the inside. Everyone called it a stroke, a heart attack. I was the only one who knew she'd simply let herself burn it all down.

Now, seventy-something years later, I'm the old lady drinking bourbon. My crepey skin glows blue, green, gold, and red next to the blinking Christmas tree with too many mismatched ornaments and tacky silver garland.

"All these Antifa thugs." Dip grunts pieces of a conversation he's been having with himself all day. He's settled into the recliner with another beer, undoing his pants and tucking his liver-spotted hand against his belly. "This country... I just don't know." His middle-aged boys, all divorced with kids they only know from every other weekend and holiday, stare at the football game on the big screen, ignoring him.

I don't want to be here. I'd had enough of them when we were together at Thanksgiving with them all muttering about what that talk radio guy said about the elections. But my idiot daughter-in-law in that reindeer sweater even though it's ninety degrees outside picked me up again. She must always draw the short straw to come get me from what everyone calls an assisted living facility but I know is a dumping ground. She deposited me on the sofa in her ugly living room like I'm a package she had to sign for.

One of Dip's grandsons—I can't keep their names straight—brought a girl this year. When we open presents, she sits on the outskirts of the family, clutching her cell phone, pretending to be interested in what's revealed in everyone else's gift boxes and bags. She had one present she opened before everyone else because the boy insisted, his voice like a toddler begging everyone to *look, look, look.*

The girl moves closer and closer to the door, fingering the new yellow gold chain with the heart pendant, a tiny stone winking in the blinking lights, keys in her other hand. I know that posture. Maybe she doesn't have a daddy at home. Maybe her mama never taught her she's worth more than a strip mall diamond chip necklace. How long have she and the boy been dating? How much of herself has she given away so far?

Sydney, the only tolerable grandchild, sidles over to me. Her older brother and cousins won't let her play some video game in the other room, and her cheeks are mottled with rage and shame. She must be eleven years old now, chubby and awkward, but with a powerful woman buried beneath the surface.

"Siddy," I say, tugging the end of her braid, "Go take my glass into the kitchen." When she leans in to take it out of my hand, I smell the sulfur just under her skin, like a secret river pulsing.

I already told her what she needed to know at her eighth birthday party. I taught her how to keep the fire low while she sat with tears trembling against her lashes, humiliated by her mother when she'd snatched a second cupcake out of the girl's hand. "You don't need that," her mother whisper-hissed, and I'd smelled the feral scent as the fire-beast in Siddy blinked awake. She walks my glass away from me, and the flames push against the back of my breastbone, just above where I carried my baby boys, a red oven that's still hot. Siddy has everything I can give her. There's no reason to keep counting to ten.

I glare at my sons, two watching their wives cleaning up and one passed out in the sun-room, just his feet showing from where they're propped up on the ottoman. I look at their wives packaging all the leftover food and cleaning every last scrap of the ribbons and wrapping paper. I drop my eyes to the little grandchildren, already bored with their new toys and the older ones taking pictures of themselves and thumbing through their phones. I wait for Siddy to return from the kitchen. She leans against the wall. Her eyes are divining rods that find fire instead of water, and they're fixed on me.

Mammaw had barely scorched the couch she'd been sitting on. I'd be doing them a favor if I ruin this one. I don't close my eyes. I catch Siddy's and hold them tight before I take a deep breath and let go.

Siren Song

She perched on a squat beach chair, holding a glass of the merlot kept just for her. Her tail was curled into a faded blue plastic kiddie pool that her favorite bartender, Ernie, brought out from the storage space near the garbage cans whenever she bobbed up in the canal behind the bar.

The brackish water Ernie'd scooped in three bucket loads for her sloshed as she shifted slightly to face the man who finally left the bar and sat down on a bench near her. Ernie's smile twisted as he watched the man put his elbows on his knees and lean in. Ernie had known all afternoon how the day would end. He knew it when the man docked his boat, the Salty Swallow, earlier and knocked back three Jack and Cokes, his shirt completely unbuttoned and flapping in the breeze made by the ceiling fan as if the man had sat on a bird that was determined to fly away.

"Why don't you sing to me? You can try to seduce me, baby."

"That's presumptuous, and kind of racist."

"Where's your snatch? Is it under all those scales?"

"Now you're just being rude."

The man scooted the bench closer and stared at her breasts, one of which sagged off to the side like a lazy eye beneath her tangled hair.

"How do you get up here from the water? Do you just flop like a fish, or what?"

"There's always someone nice enough to carry me. Are you nice, sugar?"

"Oh, I can be real nice."

She shifted toward him, and he focused on her green eyes for the first time.

~

The water was an orange mirror, reflecting the setting sun. Ernie dumped the water from the pool and held it above his head, silhouetted in front of the horizon like a god prepared to hurl a boulder. He wedged it in its space between the recycling bins and the empty kegs. He waved to her, opening and closing his fingers like a toddler saying bye-bye. By the time he was behind the bar again to finish cleaning up so he could go home, he'd wonder how the sleeves of his t-shirt had gotten so wet.

"I'll see you soon, sweetie!" She threw aside the shard of bone she'd been using to dislodge a piece of gristle from between her teeth and disappeared below the surface.

A Year After They Stopped Bothering to Name the Hurricanes

The zebra is back. Another escapee from the zoo. Who knows how it managed to survive this long? I can see it from the kitchen window where I'm washing underwear and t-shirts in the sink. The water's rotten-egg smell is worse. Everything I wear, even my skin, smells like the inside of a lunchbox left in the backseat of a hot car. It's not like I can just run down to Walmart and buy bags of salt for the well. I'm lucky to have running water at all no matter how bad it stinks.

The zebra pauses, its ears moving like antennae as it sniffs the air. Back when those prehistorically huge pythons that exploded themselves after trying to eat deer were all over social media, my Pappaw said if you tipped Florida upside-down and shook it, a whole circus's worth of animals would parade out of the Everglades. I guess the zebra's better than a giant snake, and definitely better than those goddam monkeys that came through last winter, but this guy doesn't look like a glossy National Geographic creature. I can count the ribs through its raggedy coat, and there's some kind of scabrous sore on its too-pink muzzle. It limps across my sodden back yard, nosing for grass that isn't there.

Before my whole world got blown apart, I would have tried to figure out who to call to come pick up a lost zebra or at least try to feed it a head of lettuce or something. I would have been shocked and amazed at the sight of it. I would have posted a picture on Instagram with a caption crafted over a few drafts. Now, nothing really surprises me anymore, and the zebra is just one more thing I can't afford to let break what's left of my heart.

COMMUTE

At the stoplight, I think about turning left instead of right and going who-knows-where but definitely not to my office. Then it turns green, and I move along my path just like every weekday morning. Once I merge onto the highway, the idea of turning the steering wheel ever so slightly and letting the car wander into the other lane occurs to me again. I don't want to die. A coma would be nice as long as there are no brain injuries. Maybe just a couple of broken bones and a black eye or something. I side-eye the car next to me and it's a woman with a toddler in the back seat, and she's smiling and the little boy is smiling and I'm not a monster so I just keep going.

Last night Dan said, "Let's go out!" as if getting all the stuff in the diaper bag and making sure there's something uploaded on the iPad and getting two kids in the car before we're starving and grouchy is so easy. I told him I wasn't hungry and waved at them all from the doorway.

"I'm going to get the house cleaned up," I'd said, and Dan smiled too big and said too quickly that the house could definitely use a good cleaning, so not long after they left, I was standing in the backyard with two hamsters in my hands.

"Be free," I whispered before setting them down gently on the side of the fence that the realtor called a conservation area, but we know is just a wet patch of wildness. I walked back to the house, ignoring thoughts of owls and snakes, planning on blaming the disappearance on my daughter who cried and cried and cried when I told her gently, "You must have left the cage open."

My exit is coming up, and I put on my blinker, but my gaze lifts to the sign above the endless line of red eyes staring back at me. I could head south and keep going. By four o'clock I could be in Key West where no one would care if I never wore a bra again. But I just go the way I always go. My sensible car is like that ride at Disney World, the one with the racecars. Kids grip their little steering wheels as if they really believe they could drive right to the castle if they could just find a way to get off the track. But they just go round and round on a road to nowhere.

I ride down the ramp to the gridlock of downtown toward the parking garage, hoping my spot on the third floor next to the breezeway isn't taken again today. My life narrows to a pinpoint in front of me, and I squeeze myself into it for one more day, wishing there was someone to put me on the other side of my fence.

The Morning After

The door opens downstairs, and I freeze before dropping a fistful of freshly laundered underwear into my drawer. After twenty-six years of hearing his familiar feet entering our home, I know it's not Jack, coming back for his wallet, his coffee, his keys. I'm realizing my phone is downstairs in my bag. I scan for a weapon or a place to hide when she calls out to me. Her voice in one syllable is worse than a home invasion. Worse than a serial killer picking this house at 8:07 on a Thursday morning.

I clatter down the stairs, and Meg is already at the kitchen table. Her eyes are empty blue horizons as I take the seat across the table and wait to hear about the failed exam. The huge speeding ticket. The expertly hidden drug problem. But her stillness whispers how much worse, how very much worse the circumstances are that drove her home, two hours south on the highway, and dropped her across from me. Everything inside me clenches into a fist.

She tells me, and it's a monstrous cliché. A frat house. Too much to drink. Waking up on a couch in a back room with no underwear and a blanket laid sideways across where her skirt was shoved up around her waist, her mind and thighs sticky.

We sit together while the clock on the wall ticks with a reassuring metronomic rhythm. I match my breaths to it. One, two, three—in. One, two, three—out until my face is a pool of water without a single ripple to mar its calm. Until I can reach across the table and stroke her arm with my thumb and not grip her to the bone, not try to squeeze out the poison.

Beneath the surface I am Truman with my finger on the red button. I am Edmond Dantes, crushing the lives of my enemies. I am Alex Forrest, stroking the silky rabbit fur. I am Anton Chigurh, and the coin has come up tails. I am Shiva, destroyer of worlds.

But she's a little girl again, sitting in a chair on a quiet morning, waiting for her mom to tell her what to do. The choices hang in the air between us. I want to tell her to get in the car right now. I want a rape kit. An investigation. DNA. I want every male cheek at that university swabbed and tested. I want justice, vengeance, retribution.

Meg asks if it ever happened to me, and I deflate like a balloon because I know there will be nothing that can redeem what was taken. I nod, tasting the Bartles and Jaymes wine cooler and feeling the length of my ponytail clenched in his hand. I'd crept past my mother, curled under a blanket on the couch, asleep in front of Johnny Carson while she waited for me to get home, to make sure I was safe.

That Meg would come straight home, come to me, is a bitter affirmation: I'm a good mother. I hold the thought between my teeth as I tell her I'll do whatever she wants to do. All her choices were stolen from her, and I know I have to give her this one back, an impossible, inadequate gift I hold out.

"Do I need a prescription for a morning after pill?"

I have no idea, but I tell her I'll find out.

"I just want to take a shower and go to bed."

I make my voice as still and steady as the pillow waiting for her on her bed. I tell her taking a shower will destroy evidence if she wants to file a police report.

She nods and says maybe she'll just wash her face, and she heads toward the stairs.

I pull my phone out of my bag with shaking hands and Google "rape crisis center" just in case that's what she wants to do. Then I look up "emergency contraception" to figure out where and how we can get it. I'm glad the car is full of gas and the state line is close, but the anger rises in a tsunami of rage that we have to go any farther than the pharmacy eight blocks away. I keep counting with the clock and hold back the tide. The bathroom door closes upstairs, and I hold my breath, listening for the sound of her decision.

FOUND THINGS

It was supposed to cheer her up. Hank suggested it on the way home yesterday, "Hey, babe, let's go out on the boat tomorrow and dock at that place you like for lunch."

But it was hot, the kind of hot that bleached all color from the sky and made the bay water that was already as tepid and dull as dishwater seem thicker. Even the breezes were slow and sluggish. And now Jane wished she was home in the air-conditioning, cleaning up Mark's room and feeling sorry for herself.

Yesterday had been hard. Mark had procrastinated packing, and Hank woke him up earlier than planned. Everyone's nerves were taut and stretched as thin as paper about to rip.

"I've got it under control, Dad."

"Well, no you don't. We're supposed to leave in a half hour, and not only are you not showered or dressed, but you still haven't finished packing."

"It's not like I have to be there at a specific time."

"Well, it's not like your mom and I have nothing else to do today."

Jane had fluttered through the hallway,

listening to them, trying to figure out whether she should help Mark or wait silently until it was time to go. As Hank stalked out to the garage to put down the back row of seats to make room, Mark caught his mother's eye and smirked. He looked down the hallway to make sure his father was safely in the garage before he mouthed the word, "Well," posing with his tongue on his top teeth and holding the last letter for a moment with his eyebrows raised. Jane giggled, feeling disloyal but relieved Mark was going to let her be his ally.

"Show me what's ready to be packed up." All week she'd been reminding him to get everything ready so they could move him into his dorm at UCF, and all week he'd rolled his eyes and said he'd get to it. Now it was time to go, and his room looked like it always did. There were dirty (or maybe clean?) clothes stacked on his chair and bed. A tower of plastic tumblers leaned next to his desk, and the garbage can was overflowing. The big plastic bins she'd bought at Target two weeks ago were still empty except for one that had a single towel in it.

They worked quietly. Jane lifted items along with her eyebrows, and Mark would nod, point, or shrug until the bins were more or less filled.

"Where's your inhaler?"

Mark patted his pocket. "I'm going to take a quick shower, and then we can go."

Jane turned in a slow circle after he'd gone down the hall to the bathroom, the one he'd had all to himself since his sister left for the

University of Florida three years ago. Resting on his pillow, in the middle of the unmade bed Jane would take care of later, was Mark's stuffed manatee.

He'd picked that thing out from the Tampa Zoo gift shop when he was two years old and slept with it ever since. He'd named it Zoo and referred to it with feminine pronouns until everyone else in the house talked about the blobby gray creature with fuzzy flippers as if she was a small and silent sister. Jane used to stand outside his bedroom door, left open precisely two inches, and watch his narrow chest rise and fall with Zoo tucked under his chin, fingers twined in her pink ribbon until Mark had started closing his door at night sometime in third grade.

He'd taken that ribbon between the thumb and index finger of his right hand and, starting from the bow that devolved into just a knot, pull to the end and start again. Over and over. When he couldn't fall asleep, when it thundered, when he was watching *Courage, the Cowardly Dog*, when he was doing algebra homework, his fingers were rhythmically following the line of ribbon until it was threadbare and pale as the inside of a shell left in the sun.

Zoo had gone with him the entire first week and a half of kindergarten, several sleepovers, an overnight stay in the hospital when his asthma had gotten frighteningly bad, and, most notably, a trip to Washington, D.C. at the end of eighth grade.

Now she was beached on his pillow,

marooned and bereft. Jane almost placed her in one of the bins but stopped herself. This was what she and Hank had talked about again and again. She needed to let Mark make his own decisions, run his own life. She went and sat on the living room couch to wait for Hank and Mark to pack up the car.

She and Hank followed Mark as he drove his car out of Tampa, across I-4 to Orlando. They stayed behind him when he went the wrong way on campus, executing an identical three-point turn and going back to the road they'd passed that would take them to the parking lot behind the dorm. Hank passed Mark a ten-dollar bill as a "suggested donation" to rent a cart to transport the bins, a mini fridge, and a coffeemaker to his dorm room.

His new roommate, the one Jane told Mark all of July and half of August to at least text or email, wasn't there yet. Hank stacked the bins next to a wall.

"Well," Hank said and then cleared his throat. "I'll go return the cart."

Jane opened a bin and pulled out a handful of boxer briefs, waiting for Mark to pick his side of the room so she'd know which dresser to fold them into.

"Mom." Mark took his underwear out of her hands and dropped them back in the bin. He snapped the lid shut. "I'll unpack later."

"I can make your bed."

"Mom."

Jane backed up until she was in the doorway,

watching Mark avoid her eyes until Hank returned and said, "Let's go get some lunch."

Mark locked the door with his new key. Jane reminded him to put it on his keyring so he wouldn't lose it, but he slipped it loose into his pocket, avoiding his mother's eyes.

They all got in Jane's minivan, and she realized she didn't need it anymore. She hadn't needed all that space for years. There used to be a little mirror that snapped under the bigger one so she could keep an eye on the kids in the backseat. Merry always fell asleep in the van within minutes. Mark always looked out the window. Jane would peek at him in his car seat, and he'd look up with his huge blue eyes and grin when he caught her watching him. With Hank driving, she snuck a glance into the backseat. Mark was hunched over his phone. There were no smiles for either of them.

They had lunch and went to Target where Jane kept piling stuff in the cart. Hangers, first aid kit, Clorox wipes, shower caddy, extra toothbrush, as many of Mark's favorite snacks until the cart was full. Hank swiped his card in silence. They helped Mark carry all the shopping bags into his still roommateless room. Hank slipped him two hundred-dollar bills; Jane knew he'd made a special trip to the bank three days ago on his lunch break to get them.

"We'll put money in your account each week, but it's always good to have cash," he said.

"Thanks, Dad."

Mark hugged Hank, resting his chin on top

of his dad's head, and Jane didn't think she could bear it. She crossed her arms and clutched her elbows to hold herself together.

"Well," Hank cleared his throat and turned to the hallway, "I'm going to wait out here while your mom says her goodbyes."

She clenched her hands with Mark's childhood pressed between them like something he gave her to hold for him, something to tuck into a pocket for later. Her world tipped, and she strangled a sob she could have passed as clearing her throat if she'd been quicker to think of it.

"Momma…" Mark stepped closer and put his arms around her. She clutched his shoulders, rocking slightly back and forth from foot to foot, drowning in the motion that her body knew as well as breathing.

"Don't cry, Momma."

"You left Zoo behind."

Mark laughed, put his hands on Jane's shoulders and looked down into her eyes. He picked up his backpack, unzipped it, pulled Zoo out, and touched her nose to Jane's in a proxy kiss. Jane's world righted itself momentarily.

She and Hank drove back to Tampa. They talked about Meredith's new boyfriend whom they'd not yet met, decided who would come home from work early on Wednesday to meet the pest control man, wondered if they'd be hungry for dinner later. She cried a little, and Hank handed her a paper napkin from a stash he kept in the pocket of the car door and suggested a day on the boat.

~

And there she was, facing backward because she didn't like the wind blowing directly into her face. They'd gone to the restaurant, and she'd hopped out and tied off the boat, ignoring Hank double-checking how she'd secured the rope to the cleats. She'd eaten a grouper sandwich and shifted to keep her bare thighs from sticking to the plastic covering of the seats. Now Hank was chugging through a no-wake zone, and Jane was looking at all the big boats docked along the canal as they headed back out to Tampa Bay.

As they passed the speed buoy, Hank twirled his finger in the air, signaling for Jane to hold on. He pushed down the throttle, and the front of the boat—Jane could never remember what it was supposed to be called—lifted up as they glided along the glassy water into the bay.

The sun beat down on the water, tipping the light chop with sparkling light. Jane took off her shirt and spread sunblock on her shoulders, making sure to get under the straps of her bathing suit.

She wondered what Mark was doing. If he'd gotten a good night's sleep on that little dorm bed. If he liked his roommate. If she'd like his roommate. She had never thought so much about Meredith who'd launched into the world after high school like a rocket ready to create its own orbit. Meredith was Hank's and Mark was Jane's. That's how it had been since the kids were little, and Jane knew it wouldn't always be that way. When (*if,* she corrected herself grudgingly) Meredith got married and had babies, Jane would be useful and valued again.

Hank throttled back abruptly, and Jane slid on the seat, holding herself from falling onto the deck.

"What the hell, Hank?"

"Look, babe!"

Jane followed Hank's finger and saw a pod of porpoises less than twenty yards away. Jane counted at least eighteen, breaching the water like silver rainbows. Their exhalations were the only sound in the stillness of the center of the bay. There were several young ones, rising and falling with improbably beautiful smoothness, a harmonized rhythm so perfect it hurt Jane's heart.

One of the large ones slid directly by the boat, rolling so Jane was only a few feet away from the white expanse of its belly and the liquid blackness of its eyes. It considered her with its slight smile as if she were a well-worn joke someone just told.

"I wish Merry was here," Hank whispered, and Jane smiled. Meredith marveled over every pelican's dive. Every churning school of bait fish. She would have been next to Jane, hanging onto the moment. They would have caught each other's eyes at some point and smiled, joined for a few seconds. Tears brewed in the backs of Jane's eyes. Meredith had her own life that had nothing to do with Jane, and soon Mark would too.

The porpoises moved on, dipping and resurfacing farther and farther away, the short bursts of their breath disappearing. Hank took off his hat, wiped his forehead, and put it back on.

"Do you want a water from the cooler, babe?"

Jane nodded, still searching the flat surface for the porpoises. She saw the water boiling about fifty yards away and squinted.

"Hank?"

"I only have one water. You want it, or do you want a Coke?"

"What's that?"

Jane pointed, and Hank came to stand behind her, gazing along her arm to where the water was disturbed.

"Pelican? Looks like it might be tangled in something."

"Go see."

They motored slowly until they got to where Jane had seen the disorder in the calm sheet of water. There was nothing visible, and Hank shrugged.

"Must have been a fish or..."

A creature rose and flailed as if to find a way to get a foothold on the water, scrabbling frantically.

"Oh my God! It's a dog!"

"Get the net, Janie!"

But Jane had already balanced herself on bare feet and bent from her waist over the edge of the boat, reaching down into the water. She felt Hank grab her hips to steady her before she tipped in, and she grabbed the loose skin on the back of the little dog's neck with one hand and cupped her other hand under its tail to lift the small body up and into the boat.

It lay on the bench where Jane set it, panting, its legs paddling as if it was still treading water.

"I'll be damned," Hank muttered, "It must have fallen off someone's boat."

"It doesn't have a collar or anything." Jane grabbed a towel from the other side of the bench and wrapped the dog in it, cradling it in her arms.

"Well, easy now, Janie. Don't get bitten."

She rubbed the towel over the damp head, gently smoothing hair away from the black eyes.

"What kind of mutt do you think that is?" Hank handed Jane the bottle of water he'd gotten from the cooler. "See if you can get it to drink."

Jane poured a little into her hand. The dog lapped it up and licked her fingers greedily. She poured out a little at a time until the dog wiggled in her arms to be released. It stood on the bench and shook itself thoroughly before considering the damp towel Jane had set down. It pawed it, moving the folds around before circling four times like casting a private spell and dropping into the perfection of the center. It looked up at Jane briefly before resting its head on the towel and closing its eyes.

"I wonder how long it's been out there," Jane said, running her hand along the coarse fur.

Hank lifted up one of the dog's hind legs, eliciting only a brief look of reproach through slitted eyes. "It's a she. She couldn't have been treading water too long. An hour at most with those little legs."

"Who'd lose their dog and not realize it?" Jane was suddenly furious at the careless eyes that had not been watching diligently.

"Well, you're assuming it was an accident, babe."

Jane opened her mouth and shut it, stunned into silence by the vision of someone picking up the little dog, throwing it into the water, and speeding away without looking back to see the brown head bobbing in the waves.

"Let's head back to the marina and figure this all out." Hank restarted the boat and motioned for Jane to hang onto the dog.

She carefully pulled the towel into a bundle and settled the dog on her lap before the engines snarled the silence away. They had about twenty minutes at full speed and then another twenty to get through the no-wake zone approaching the marina. Jane turned to shade the dog from the sun with her body, and the dog shifted and rested her chin on Jane's wrist, looking up at her with a certainty of trust that made Jane dizzy. She stroked the narrow head, smiling as the wiry hair dried and began to fluff.

"Don't you name her," Hank said once he'd throttled back to idle speed as they entered the channel.

"I haven't named her."

"Well, that's someone's dog."

"Really? Someone who either threw her overboard or didn't even notice when she fell?"

Hank sighed and gazed over Jane's head toward the next channel marker. The engine growled quietly as the water slapped the sides of the boat.

They'd had a dog when they first married, a silver-muzzled lab mix Jane found scavenging around a garbage can in the Publix parking lot. She'd coaxed it into her car with a handful of cocktail peanuts. Hank had grimaced, protesting they didn't have time for a dog. Jane simply didn't respond to anything Hank said, no matter how reasonable. It was Hank who took the dog they'd dubbed Gravy to the vet three years later and came back gripping the empty collar, sobbing. There'd been no other dogs.

Hank maneuvered the boat toward the dock. Jane slipped her left arm under the dog's belly, cradling her like a football, and pulled the towel around her little body.

"While I finish up, why don't you ask around and see if anyone knows anything about a missing dog?"

Jane glared at Hank, and he watched her make her way up the dock, clutching the dog and the towel. She gave the two people she passed a wide berth, angling her body away from them as if protecting herself from wind. Hank rubbed his chin as Jane vanished into the parking lot.

"Hey, Dan." Hank raised a hand to the marina employee approaching in the forklift. "I'll be ready in just a minute. Can you hose it out for me today while you're flushing the engine? I've got to get going."

Dan nodded. "Y'all didn't by any chance see a dog out there today, did you? Some guy called a while back. Said he's been calling all the marinas. They found a stray pup on the road and took it out on the boat with them. Thing must have fallen off, and they forgot they even had it on board. He feels bad, and his wife is pissed, so I guess he was hoping someone might've found it."

Hank picked up their cooler and swung it onto the dock. He spotted Jane, still clutching the dog, by their car. "Nope," he said, climbing out of the boat, "We didn't see anything. Hope it's okay."

Before Hank left the marina parking lot and accelerated onto the road, he looked at his wife. The dog was curled in her lap, and Hank reached out to trail his fingers down Jane's cheek before he stroked the little dog's ears.

"We could name her Salty," he said.

Jane smiled and shifted the dog so she could rest her left hand on Hank's right knee as they headed home.

CARLINE

As soon as she gets in the car, she's crying, and I ask what's wrong, and she just says, "Nothing," and I say nothing because I already know what's wrong because what's wrong has been wrong for weeks and this is far from the first time she's run past the teacher on duty, waving goodbye to no one because no one is waving goodbye to her, and I look out the window at the girls laughing with their arms linked and their hair glossy, and their long-limbed perfection makes me want to turn the wheel and run right through the group of them, and they're laughing, laughing, laughing, and I know that sound so well, and it would be so easy for me to hurt them, not even with my car but with words I've sharpened for years since my words were blunt and dull when I needed them most for myself, but I don't turn the wheel because I know my girl just wants them to say something nice to her, and turning the wheel wouldn't help my crying girl crumpled in the backseat of my car, the one who tells the dog "bless you" if he sneezes, the one who sticks just the tip of her tongue out when she colors or does jigsaw puzzles, the one who can sing along with any '80s song because she says that's the decade of her spirit, and she just wants those other girls to see her and smile and maybe, just maybe, say, "See you tomorrow," and give her a reason, one I can't give, to dry her eyes.

OUT OF THE WOODS

The humidity was as thick as a wet wool blanket and the mosquitoes she bothered to slap made bloody freckles on her arms and legs, but Ellen stayed outside with her dog past midnight. Bunco sat by her side, fanning his tail like a windshield wiper across the pool deck, his broad head tilted up at her. She already checked to make sure the kick hadn't done any damage. He wasn't limping or acting like he was hurt. "He didn't mean it," she lied, and Bunco put one heavy paw on her knee. She smiled, stroking the scarred head where the dog's ears used to be.

The rescue lady said they were probably cut off, common for dogs forced to fight. Ellen filled out the paperwork, skin hot and hands shaking, after hearing that detail. She drove home with Bunco's head out the window, a line of drool like a kite string flying behind his smile. Even after six years, Eric still called Bunco "freak dog" and refused to feed, refill his water dish, or take him out if she had to work late.

When she came out of the kitchen earlier to ask Eric if he was hungry for dinner, she caught him racing from the bathroom back to his video game, kicking Bunco out of his way. Ellen felt the shift inside her head when the dog yelped and curled like a comma as he crept to her side. There was a realization, like a lightbulb over a cartoon character's head. She went from *I can put up with it* to *oh, hell no.*

"I was just getting him to move," Eric said, never taking his eyes off the screen where he shot and killed the online versions of other grown-ass men. But he'd never actually hurt Bunco before, that she knew of.

The dog walked to the edge of the pool, looking down into the twelve or so inches of stagnant rainwater at the bottom where tadpoles swarmed like dirty sperm. There was a leak that she'd tried to get fixed, but then Eric lost his job, and everything was so expensive, and they didn't even use the pool anymore anyway. Ellen shoved to her feet and walked to the edge of the deck. It was getting harder to tell where their yard ended, and the swampy conservation area began because their grass needed mowing. That was one of the things that they'd agreed to back when they'd first bought the house. Eric was supposed to mow every week and take the garbage can to the curb Tuesdays and Fridays.

Those jobs, like his gig work, had become less frequent. Just yesterday, Ellen rolled the overflowing and stinky garbage can behind his car, almost touching the bumper. It was in the same spot when she got home. It was only the thought of Bunco, who probably hadn't been taken out all day, that convinced her to go inside to confront Eric. But she'd stared at his slack face, pointed toward the TV, and walked past him. Once outside, Bunco peed for almost a minute.

Tonight, the woods were full of owls screaming like tortured monkeys. Rustling palmettos transformed passing turtles and opossums into invisible dinosaurs. Live oaks and pine trees blocked out the moon. When the realtor showed them the house for the first time, Eric peered into the woods and muttered, "It's kind of creepy out there."

But Ellen loved being able to walk to the edge of such wildness, psychotic owl screams and all. That was back when she still thought happiness would be easy. Back when all the little things that bothered her about Eric would never be big things.

Since then, the years slithered away. Six years of Ellen managing a small law firm office that specialized in defending drunk drivers and deadbeat dads. Four years since Eric said he didn't want children. Ever. Two years since a "misunderstanding" cost him his teaching job. A year and a half of him half-assedly driving for Uber and Lyft. A month since she discovered the text on his phone he claimed was "nothing." Three weeks fantasizing about driving into a new life with Bunco, his drool flying out the window. Forty-five minutes of contemplating how much she'd hate herself if she stayed.

Something moved in the shadows. Gooseflesh erupted across her skin. Probably just an armadillo, but she felt watched. Felt *seen*. Bunco stood at the edge of the grass and sniffed the air. The evening was quiet, still. The black smell of standing water, teeming with mosquito larvae and rot, hovered like another layer of shadow.

She squinted into the woods that would have been perfect for a child to feed squirrels and find deer tracks in the soft earth. Later, the child could play manhunt with neighborhood kids, hiding behind a tree and trying to swallow the fear that could rattle bones when everyone else had been found.

But the sidewalks in this neighborhood never rang with the sounds of *no, you're it!* Or splashing echoes from backyard pools. The kids were indoor creatures, and Ellen didn't have a child to join them even if they ventured outside. She looked deeper into the darkness, between the trees. She imagined a girl, waiting for her, holding out a hand to lead her into a different direction like a coin pressed in her palm. A girl with her own eyes but with a hopeful future, ready for her to find.

She couldn't follow that child into the woods, but she could make another path to her. She didn't need to stay in this house. She could find a new wildness. Ellen patted her thigh for Bunco to follow. Eric wouldn't even notice. Her absence would just be one more thing left sitting behind him, close but never touching.

TUESDAY

Everything in the detox unit is white, including my anger. It bleeds into the love for Clay like bleach on red fabric, staining it, changing it, robbing it of color, ruining it. I don't want to be here, but there was no way I couldn't come. I'm always the one my brother calls. I spoke with him last night on the phone for his allotted five minutes. He'd told me he was cold, but the nurse won't let me bring him a hoodie or the blanket. I can't have anything when I enter the unit. Not my phone, not my purse, not even my car keys. I should have remembered from the last time he wound up in the ER, but that was almost a year ago.

My hostility radiates heat, but there's guilt underneath it all, an acknowledgment that my resentment of this inconvenience and my shame is misplaced. *It's a disease* I remind myself once again, but I've never quite convinced myself of that. *It's a choice* the anger hisses.

The orderly who buzzes me in looks like anyone and no one in his blue scrubs. Behind him on the white linoleum two patients shuffle across the wide hallway in their grippy-bottomed socks. The man looks at me briefly and then turns and hurries back the way he came. He could be thirty or sixty and has the broken capillaries around his eyes and nose and the bloat of a drunk.

The girl looks like a teenager, and I try to imagine her in a high school chemistry or geometry class. She'd have flawless makeup from watching tutorials on YouTube, and her hair would be glossy and perfect. She drifts by me under the fluorescent lights, and I see a long string of drool swinging from her slack mouth. I watch to see if she will wipe it off or if it will land on her baby blue hospital robe and pull away from her lip. It just hangs, and I focus on it until I see Clay come around the corner and shamble toward me.

The cut on his forehead from where he was a literal falling-down drunk two nights ago when I brought him to the hospital is still livid and pitiful. Every time he gets hurt without dying is a bitter miracle. He's forty-two, only eighteen months older than me, but he looks like an old man. He needs a shave, and his eyes aren't right, unfocused and unseeing. Valium, I guess. Maybe Ativan.

Wrath vibrates inside me, gripping my ribs in its fists as it shakes and shakes, but being angry at this wreck of a man is like being angry at the aftermath of a tornado. His hands tremble, and his eyes cast around, searching for something that isn't immediately under his fingers. He's always looking for something—his car keys, five dollars, an excuse someone might believe. I'm always just looking for him.

My anger is useless to both of us, so I take a deep breath and walk toward him with my arms open. He rests his hands lightly on my back as I press my cheek against his chest, trying to ignore the sour stench of his unwashed skin and the tightness of my throat where I hold my tears. He pats once, twice, a third time, and the embrace is over. He's tolerated the explicit excess of my love long enough.

We go to a room filled with what looks like garage sale furniture, including one of those spring-exhausted couches I know will swallow me if I dare to sit on it. We lower ourselves instead onto straight-backed chairs, thigh to thigh, at a card table. Side by side is good. I can't stand looking at his ruined face or those lightless eyes. He might actually talk to me if he doesn't have to see himself reflected back in mine.

All I want to do is leave and never come back, go home where my husband waits to ask, "How *is* he? How are *you?* Where my kids are finishing homework, texting friends, wondering idly where I've been. I could leave, and no one would judge me, but I know no one else will come in my place.

I have so many words that could crumple him like an old receipt, but I reach past them for a stack of puzzle boxes balanced on the edge of the table beside my elbow. I take the top one—an underwater scene—and shake the pieces out. I find the corners and fit the straight-edged pieces together for the border. I ask him questions I'd ask a toddler: *What did you eat today? Are the people here nice?* He answers like a teenager: *Nothing. I don't know.*

He stops answering, not ignoring me as much as simply going somewhere the medication has taken him. The silence is more comfortable anyway. I fill in the dolphin and start looking for pieces with black and white for the killer whale. He pushes several pieces toward me, and the hands of the clock on the wall keep moving. Blue water. Yellow reef fish. Green turtle. Gray shark. An orange and white clown fish.

When all the pieces are connected, there are holes in the scene. I press my fingers on either side of my eyes and relax my jaw, so I don't turn my molars to dust. Someone should have just thrown the damn thing away. I check the floor, but no pieces had fallen. I grip the side of the table with both hands to keep myself from flipping it over just to see all the pieces scatter. I want to scream and flail and kick. I want to bite and scratch and rip flesh.

Clay peers at the dingy tile as if he's still searching for the missing pieces, but his eyes are at a deep depth I can't fathom. He can't see what's in front of him. I fill my lungs and ease the breath out until I can unclench my fingers. I take the puzzle apart, putting every piece back in the box, and then I set the box on the top of the stack where I found it.

He rubs a hand through his hair, and the white line of an old scar shines on his forehead. He pushed me higher and higher in the wooden swing that hung from the jacaranda tree in our backyard. Our voices were the sounds of summer, the smell of the mosquito truck we'd follow on our bikes so we could stay out and not get eaten alive, the taste of homemade popsicles. I went too high, and the corner of the seat crashed into his skull, splitting the skin. It's only one little mark, nothing compared to all the ones I'll never see, but it's him, and it's me, and we're us.

My eyes burn as I push myself out of the chair and tell him I have to go. He lists to his feet like a boat taking on water and moves six slow steps to a sign posted on the wall. *Visiting hours: 6p.m.– 8p.m. Tuesday and Thursday.* He looks back at me, tapping the last word until I nod. He wants me to come back. All the hurt, all the disappointment, all the anger recedes instantly. It all goes, leaving nothing behind except the space between us, filled with the echo of my feet kicking toward the sky and the certainty he'd always catch me.

A Whole Universe

In the end, Pete couldn't do it. Kara wasn't surprised. She knew his fear—of the flight, of the hibernation, of starting over, of so many things—was inexplicably stronger than the fear of what the news outlets had been calling "certain planetary annihilation." Still, she'd booked one of the last shuttles to give him as much time as possible to decide death was heavier than fear.

Sam and their daughter, Taylor, left weeks ago, right after Kara was notified they'd won four spots in the lottery. Before they left, Sam whispered, "No matter what, you get on that ship. Promise me."

And Kara promised. And she meant it. But when she and Pete were almost to the front of the queue, their entire lives stuffed in the one bag each person was permitted, Pete stepped quietly out of line. Kara knew the promise had been broken all along.

"Just go, Momma. I want you to go."

She buried her nose under the chin of her man-child. The yeasty scent captured there took her back twenty years to the baby she'd had alone and loved with a ferocity that made her love for Sam and even for Taylor seem painted in pale pinks while her tie to Pete pulsed with the red of fresh blood. Her sweet boy, tall and strong but fragile as a hothouse orchid. He must have thought she was saying goodbye until she stepped back and said, "You stay, I stay."

He followed her through the crowds, begging her to go back, to leave. They passed the security guard telling the weeping woman she couldn't take her dog, to the exit where lines of unlucky people waited for a miracle. Kara saw a young mother with a toddler on her hip and felt that ghost weight settle on her own body.

"I don't know if they'll let you use them, but here." She pressed their boarding cards into the woman's palm, making the decision irrevocable. She walked back to Pete and took his face in her hands. "It's done. Let's go."

He stopped arguing.

"What should we do?" He looked at her with the same wide blue eyes that she'd gazed into every time his panic rose like a tide, and she'd told him to take deep breaths, to count to ten, to trust she'd never leave him.

They'd never make it back to their house. Kara's mind was an overfilled cup of screams and cries and lights and people. She drew a slow breath, steadying herself.

"Let's walk over there." She pointed to a shipyard on the other side of the tarmac, filled with decommissioned shuttles, their noses to the sky like tombstones. "That one," Kara said, as they passed a vessel that towered like a sky-scraper, "looks like one of the first pilgrim ships.

Remember that? We watched it go up from our driveway. You told everyone at school you were going to ride one someday."

"I'm so sorry—"

"And you kept a schedule of the transports, and we'd drive out to the coast and watch them go up whenever we could."

Pete nodded and slipped his hand around Kara's. It was getting colder as a huge, black cloud devoured the sun, promising one of the storms that were a daily event since The Break. Kara shivered.

"There's a light over there." Pete pointed to a shed. "The electricity must still be on." The door hung from its hinges like a loose tooth. Inside, there were huge bolts and screws scattered on the floor and a single-bulb lamp, a coffee maker with no pot, and a toaster oven on the counter. Pete set his bag on the concrete and plugged in the oven, grinning as it glowed orange, a personal-sized sun they both moved toward like gravity.

He cleared a spot on the floor by scuffing his feet and set the toaster down. "Here, Momma," he said and took her bag so she could ease herself against the wall. Pete sat next to her and angled the oven toward them. They were already on another planet, away from the chaos on the other side of the shipyard.

"How long?" Pete whispered.

Kara's answer was to take his hand in both of hers and rub heat into his fingers before taking the other one and doing the same. He kissed the top of her head and then leaned his cheek against it.

"We'd stand by the water," he said. "You always brought a juice box and fruit snacks for me, and we'd sit on the sand and watch the launches until we couldn't see the shuttles anymore."

"The water looked like it was on fire from the boosters."

"And after you married Sam, we'd still go by ourselves."

"Because it was ours."

The toaster oven turned off. Pete leaned forward and twisted the timer again. The heat crept back out, and Kara almost believed that if she closed her eyes, she could ride back in time and cradle Pete in the silence of early morning hours. His dimpled hand would curl around her finger as he nursed, and her tiny apartment was a world in which only the two of them existed. A phantom ache moved through her breasts as the smell of his infant scalp filled her mind.

A low rumble shook the ground. They both looked up at the distant fire filling the doorway, like a painting of a future that wasn't theirs. "They're going," Pete said, reclaiming his mother's hand.

Kara lost count of the shuttles arrowing into the sky. It would be months before Sam would stand with Taylor, looking for them. He'd wait long after the last people passed through whatever checkpoints or customs they had up there. The hope would fade like the contrails Kara and Pete were watching. He'd be angry. He might teach Taylor to hate her. He'd never understand her citizenship had always been in this tiny universe next to her boy.

ONE SMALL WORLD

"Do this, Mammaw."

I guide Bean's dimpled hands, help him roll the pink doh. We shape snowmen and snakes. He smashes a little house I'd made and laughs, a gleeful destroyer of worlds.

We're being quiet so Sara can sleep. She works too hard, trying to find a way to remake her own home, her own life. Besides, she has no patience for these small architectures. The work of building a person is so slow.

I smell the top of Bean's head, the hair I washed last night that already smells like a handful of sweaty pennies, and time slips. I'm sitting at a table with my grandfather, and we're making snakes and snowmen but mostly a line of burgers and cakes and other flat, round foods because I like to play restaurant.

Back in this time, at this table with Bean, I lift my hands to my face. They smell of my childhood, like the inside of an empty glass of beer that sat on a counter overnight. I used to sneak bites of doh into my mouth, trying to make the pies and pizzas real. The saline musk with a hint of vanilla is the taste of who I was before I knew I would need to be anything else.

My hands are starting to look like my mother's. The woman who greeted me in the bathroom mirror this morning bears no resemblance to the one who lives in my head. The gray hairs are multiplying, spreading, and the lines around my eyes are from worry, not laughter. The little boy by my side is a beautiful, fragile beast who's transformed my own baby girl into a stranger whose face is achingly familiar. The only material we have to create our lives is what we already have. So, I take a big chunk, of the yellow this time, and start to squish and pull.

"What making?"

But I don't answer because I don't know yet. My knuckles push into the softness, and the pads of my fingers roll and stretch and build. I form a body. Bean's hands still as he watches me, a zealot before his god, as I create what didn't exist before. His eyes are round with wonder, and I want to be him, amazed by a simple act that ultimately means nothing. I knead and press and add long ears and a round tail.

When the creature is complete, I smile at the boy, and then smash the lumpy creature into a pancake on the table. Bean raises his eyes to mine, confused by my destruction of things, a province he thought was his alone. Like a vampire sliding a long finger along the line of a slender throat, I slip a salty bit from what was a bunny into my mouth. Bean is so beautiful that I want to crush the world around him. Instead, I press the doh against my teeth with my tongue and feel it disintegrate.

THE MAENAD

I would not have looked back. I would not have needed to turn to know she was behind me. But he was always turning back, looking from the edges of his eyes, trying to find hers, making sure they were always on him.

My beautiful sister. Gentle but also quick to laugh. There was no question Orpheus would choose her. Eurydice with the soft eyes and hair like banked embers, flashing fire from its depths. Eurydice who taught me to play, to sing, to pray because Mother died birthing me and Father never took another wife. Eurydice. The only woman I ever needed to show me what it would be to sail the currents men marked in the world.

I'd not yet bled before Eurydice was wed to smiling Orpheus with his lyre and his eyes seeking her always. Even as they stood with clasped hands, Eurydice's face shining and sure, his eyes were seeking her.

Of course he looked back. I could not give thanks for his efforts. I would not honor the journey he made to bargain cruel Hades for her return. He looked back, and I lost her again.

His tears offended me. What right did he have to mourn when he was the instrument of her loss? My tears were righteous. My anger just. And when I prayed, it was Dionysus who answered with new sisters who helped me forget with wine and music and quieted my anger with sweat and blood.

For a time, I forgot weak, faithless Orpheus as I danced with my sisters through forests and fields: homeless, husbandless, free. But when I heard his grief, drawn from the strings of his lyre, I turned with the ears of a hare, the fangs of a wolf.

I tracked him to a glen. The moon rose over me like a woman arching her back, and my sisters were a gathering storm behind me. Dionysus awakened my fury with a gentle finger that caressed music into my bones until my soul broke open in ecstasy. The night smelled of fennel's bitter sweetness and the earthy musk of snakes. My sisters and I stepped together from the shadows, like clouds streaking across a hectic sky. Orpheus became the doe. I saw him see me, measure the space between us, and find me beneath the dirt, the sweat, the blood.

"Thea?"

But I was no longer that girl, the one who laughed and lived. I was hands and teeth and hunger. I was the voice that cried, "Euoi!" to the wind, carrying the word like a prayer to my god who watched us from afar and smiled.

When my sisters and I finally staggered away, drunk and glutted with our god, I could still feel the fragile heart I'd crushed between my palms. Taste the blood. No, I was not that girl. I was simply the one who'd never look back.

CROSSING UNITED

I told her I'd meet her outside my office. And now there she is, three blocks away, standing in the stingy shade at the edge of the sidewalk, gesturing grandly below an authentic smile. She's holding court with three men as if she's balancing a tiara atop her blonde wig. They're the same men who'd stared with accusing, sullen eyes even after I'd dropped dollars in each of their cups. Now they're unfurled like blossoms, welcoming a butterfly in their midst. My mother has that terrible power to win over even the most begrudging of admirers. She's a windswept siren, a low-hanging olive branch, reality TV.

I loved her for about twelve years and then took twenty more to learn to love her again. She taught me to never leave the house without lipstick or shame. She managed bad grades, betrayals, hangovers, and broken hearts by pecking at my idle sorrow and throwing me out of the nest to fulfill her mantra of simply not thinking about difficult things. Staying busy was the answer to everything.

In her years as a widow, she's grown into someone new. I grieved the loss of my father as I slipped against my will into the edges of the space he left behind. What started as a care, a chore, a duty, turned into something else with Mom. We spend time together voluntarily: a movie, a trip to the mall, a ride to nowhere on a Sunday afternoon, a long lunch on a weekday.

Sometimes the mom I avoided for years peeks out. "Is your iron broken? I can loan you mine, so you don't look like you just crawled out of bed." Or, "We can split the flan. You don't need to eat a whole one." But the flame that used to flare and consume every good feeling is now banked and smolders listlessly without a single spark. I just smile and ask her about her new sneakers or tell her about a TV show she might like. I've stopped being surprised by my lack of anger.

She waves goodbye to her new friends as we head to lunch. One of them blows her a kiss. She blushes, and I can see the girl I never met. Her hand, as soft and loose as an old handkerchief, reaches for mine as we cross the street. I close my fingers gently around hers and tuck her against me. I am protecting her from speeding cars, stiff winds, and the vicious pavement cracks and edges that can and have sent her sprawling, that have broken bones and shed blood. I hold her hand the way she held my tiny one as we made our way through my childhood, desperate to keep everything that matters from slipping out of our grasp.

ACKNOWLEDGMENTS

I'm so grateful to my new friends at EastOver Press, including Keith Lesmeister, Walter Robinson, Beth Gilstrap, and Kelly March as well as the rest of the team who chose to make this book something I could hold in my hands.

Thanks also to the incredible Yale Writers' Workshop community, especially Jotham Burrello who helped make this opportunity possible and the other fabulous instructors I've gotten to work with, including Kirsten Bakis, Sarah Darer Littman, and Amy Shearn.

I appreciate all the incredible flash writers who inspire and teach me through their words. There are way too many to name, but I keep going back to Christopher Allen, Timothy Boudreau, Tara Campbell, Courtney Clute, Tommy Dean, Kathy Fish, Hannah Grieco, L Mari Harris, Kristin Tenor, and Cathy Ulrich.

Huge thanks to my University of South Florida family who challenge and inspire me. Rita Ciresi introduced me to flash fiction and helped me find space for my voice in the small containers of that form. She's the teacher every writer should aspire to deserve. John Fleming, my intrepid thesis director and writing sensei, and professors extraordinaire Julia Koets, Jarod Rosello, Heather Sellers, and Jake Wolff have also all been steady sources of instruction and encouragement.

I'm also thankful for my brilliant MFA cohort, including Hal Dietrich, Destiny Howell, Jade Jemison,

Rachel Knox, Erin Olds, Thomas Page, and Elisabeth Parker along with the rest of the community, especially Nikki Lyssy who always says yes when I ask if she has time to read something.

Love to Jenn Gilgan, my long-time writing partner, who is a great reader, writer, and editor and an even better friend. Her developmental feedback and sharp eye for line edits have made my work, including this book, so much stronger.

Even bigger love to Jenni Layman who is my honorary sister, best friend, and most dedicated and enthusiastic supporter.

I wish my father, Delane Pearson, was still around to enjoy this with me, but his love and pride live on, and I feel them alongside the constant love from my gorgeous mama, Audrey Pearson. I have a whole cheering squad in our little family, including my brother Darren, Aunt Myrna, Aunt Cookie, Uncle Tom, Jack, JoAnn, and the bright light of Cheri who is always with me. My kids, Pearson, Reilly, and Delaney, don't always get what I'm doing, but they always have hugs for their uncool mom, even in public.

Above all, start to finish, I'm so grateful for the guy who's been walking me home since we were beautiful, dumb teenagers. Jason's love and support are proof that there are things in this world that just don't break.

PUBLICATIONS

With gratitude to the literary journals/magazines and the editors that first gave some of my stories a home:

"Bouquets" *The Dead Mule School of Southern Literature*—November 2019

"Burning" *The Dying Dahlia*—September 2019

"Commute" *Lost Balloon*—January 2020

"Delayed Combustion" *Sledgehammer*—December 2021

"Entropy" *Rowan Glassworks*—May 2021

"The Hands Remember" *X-R-A-Y Literary Magazine*—February 2020

"Lovebugs" *Cease, Cows*—May 2020

"The Morning After" *Jellyfish Review*—May 2019

"Murmurations" *Every Day Fiction*—June 2021

"Sixth Period" *Spelk*—July 2019

"The Third Date" *Crack the Spine*—May 2019

"To-Do List" *Prometheus Dreaming*—May 2019

"A Year After They Stopped Bothering to Name the Hurricanes" *Wingless Dreamer*—February 2019

ABOUT THE AUTHOR

ANDREA RINARD was an award-winning high

school English teacher
before becoming a student
in the University of South
Florida's MFA program
where she teaches com-
position and creative writing. Her flash and micro
fiction have been featured
in such places as *X-R-A-Y Literary Magazine; Cease,
Cows; The Jellyfish Review,* and the *Short Story Today*
podcast, and her work has been nominated for Best
of the Net and Best Small Fictions. She won the 2020
Key West Literary Seminar's Marianne Russo Award
for a novel in progress. She's currently working on
her next project, a novel steeped in the history of
her native Florida where she lives with her 1988
prom date. Visit her online at www.writerinard.com.

Explore more short fiction published by

EASTOVER
— PRESS —
www.EastOverPress.com

You Have Reached Your Destination
Louise Marburg
"Marburg's characters find themselves in lives they
don't quite recognize, searching for signposts that can
lead them forward or tell them who they are...
These characters are as quirky as they are full of heart."
—*THE NEW YORK TIMES*

❧

All the Rivers Flow into the Sea & Other Stories
Khanh Ha
From Vietnam to America, this collection, jewel-like,
evocative, and layered, brings to readers a unique sense of love
and passion alongside tragedy and darker themes of peril.

❧

The EastOver Anthology of Rural Stories
First in a series, this stunning collection of short fiction by
rural & small town writers of color is evocative and engaging.

❧

The Cutleaf Reader
Our annual print anthologies collect works by numerous
established and emerging writers as published in *Cutleaf*,
our literary journal of short stories, essays, and poetry.
(www.CutleafJournal.com)

CPSIA information can be obtained
at www.ICGtesting.com
Printed in the USA
BVHW041950160523
664275BV00003B/68

9 781958 094303